The Wedding

Compass Key, book seven

Maggie Miller

THE WEDDING: Compass Key, book 7
Copyright © 2022 Maggie Miller

Second chances do exist.

Five former sorority sisters, all in their 50's, undertake the adventure of a lifetime when a mysterious invite reunites them at an exclusive resort set on a private island.

And what adventures they've had so far at Mother's! With a new section of the resort open and operating, numerous new guests, and two weddings about to take place, the women have their hands full.

Can they juggle everything that's going on in their lives and business and still produce two amazing weddings?

Walk down the aisle with them on Compass Key and find out.

Chapter One

*A*manda smoothed down her Mother's Resort shirt in anticipation of the arriving guests and smiled as the doors to the lobby opened. Check-ins were always an interesting experience and she looked forward to them. It was a chance to really meet the guests and to solidify the good impression that had already begun on their boat ride to the private island. To show them that Mother's was going to be even better than they imagined.

Or, in the case of returning guests, to remind them of just how special their experience was going to be.

It was a given that Mother's was a pretty impressive place. A luxurious, exclusive resort set on a private island that had once been the home of a famous pirate. Hard not to be impressed by at least one of those attributes.

But there was no substitute for the human touch, and that was where Amanda believed the front desk had an opportunity to build on the welcome the guests already received from the boat captain who'd brought them to Compass Key.

The couple approaching now, Conrad and Julia Heston, weren't anyone she'd known of previously, like some of the celebrity guests, but everyone was treated like a star at Mother's.

She'd Googled them. Anything she could do to learn more about incoming guests and find ways to accommodate their needs and make them happy, she did. Within reason. She wasn't about to do background checks or anything like that.

Google had told her Conrad was a freelance journalist, who, according to his blog, was writing a book on the rise of tech in modern society, and Julia worked for a firm that specialized in environmental law. Amanda wasn't sure what such a firm did, but it sounded important. As best as she could find, they had no children, but Julia had posted numerous pictures on her Instagram account of a small white dog named Charlie.

As in Charlton Heston? Whether or not that had been intentional, it was amusing all the same.

She smiled broadly. "Welcome to Mother's."

Conrad didn't smile but Julia did. The pretty blonde said, "Thanks. Happy to be here."

"We're happy to have you. I understand this is your first visit to Mother's."

Julia nodded. "It is. Really looking forward to some downtime."

"If you need anything at all, don't hesitate to ask." Amanda put a little paperwork on the countertop in front of them. "We want your stay to be as wonderful as possible."

"So do I. I read online that you do a lot of weddings here. Will there be any during our stay?" Julia sighed, her eyes going sort of moony. "I just love weddings."

There was Katie and Owen's wedding in three days, but that wasn't going to be on the island and besides, they'd all been sworn to secrecy in an attempt to keep the paparazzi at bay. Amanda shook her head. "No, I'm sorry. There's one in about two weeks, though."

"Oh. Bummer," Julia said. She leaned in. "Anyone famous?"

Amanda laughed softly. That wasn't information she would have shared, but she shook her head anyway. "No. The daughter of one of the owners."

"Oh." Julia seemed disappointed.

Conrad glanced up at Amanda quickly before picking up the pen she'd included with the paperwork. Except, he didn't sign. Instead, he seemed to actually be reading it. Most guests just scrawled their signature, eager to be on their way. As she watched him, she looked him over, noticing his watch while she did. It was habit now, to inspect the guests in a certain way. It was part of how she read them and got to know a little bit more about them.

When it came to high-end accessories, she'd found women favored purses, jewelry, shoes, and sunglasses. Men typically went for watches, belts, and sunglasses. Shoes, too, but not as much as women. And occasionally she'd see a man with a very expensive pen or a particularly upscale phone case.

She'd learned pretty quickly that the well-to-do not only liked fancy things, they liked their fancy things to be noticed.

Julia was carrying a striking hot-pink bag with the distinctive Louis Vuitton logo on the front.

Amanda gave the bag a nod. "Lovely handbag."

"Thank you." Julia glanced at her husband, who was still looking over the paperwork. "Conrad got it for me for my thirty-fifth birthday."

"What a nice present," Amanda said.

Julia seemed pleased. She wiggled her fingers at the engagement ring on Amanda's hand. "That's quite a sparkler you're wearing."

Amanda's smile broadened. "Thank you. I got engaged at Christmas."

"How fun! Now *that's* a present," Julia said with a bright grin.

"I couldn't agree more." Duke had really surprised Amanda twice on Christmas. Once with his proposal and a second time by bringing in her mother. She and her mom had done a lot of talking that evening, and while their relationship still had a long way to go, they continued to communicate, and Amanda believed things would steadily improve.

Enough so that her mother might even come to their wedding in the fall. At least her sister would come, that much Amanda knew for sure. And Amanda's children, who'd both visited the previous month.

Amanda looked at Conrad's watch again. It was a Rolex Submariner, but there was something not quite right about it. Maybe it was a vintage piece. She wasn't as familiar with those as she was the newer ones.

She couldn't figure it out, but it wasn't that important. The guest experience was what mattered. "If there's anything you'd like to do while you're here, take one of the boat cruises or enjoy some spa time, including your complimentary massage, I'd be happy to help you set that up as well. Of course, you can do that from your room phone, too if you'd like."

Conrad finally scrawled his name on the indicated lines, the muscles in his jaw tight, like he was clenching his teeth. "We're just here to relax. And be left alone."

Well, *he* was a little ray of sunshine. Amanda smiled as if he was the loveliest guest she'd ever encountered. "Absolutely."

She slid two keycards across the countertop toward them. "Bungalow 19. Ramon will escort you and your bags will be along shortly. Enjoy your stay."

Ramon was standing right behind them. He greeted the couple, then gestured toward the doors that would take them toward their bungalow.

Amanda held her smile as they departed. Her face relaxed when the doors closed behind them. Except for her brows, which pulled together as her eyes narrowed. There was something odd about those two. Well, not so much about Julia, but Conrad. He didn't act like a man on vacation. He was too uptight for that. Although maybe that was exactly why he needed to be here.

Carissa came back from the errand she'd just run

for a guest, which had been to check the boutique to see what brands of sunscreen they carried. "You look perturbed. Everything okay?"

Amanda's brows rose. "Everything's fine. Just thinking."

"About?"

"The couple that just checked in. There was something odd about them. About him, really. And I can't put my finger on what it was except that he didn't seem like a man on vacation at an exclusive resort."

Carissa shrugged. "Maybe that's exactly why he's here. To become a man on vacation."

"I thought the same thing myself. But how stressed out do you have to be to come to a place like this and still not be relaxed? The boat ride over should help, shouldn't it?"

"Maybe. So long as being on the water doesn't scare you." Carissa seemed to ponder that. "Although why would you come to a resort on a private island if you didn't like the water? That seems counterproductive."

"I agree," Amanda said. "Except maybe his wife really wanted to come and he's just doing it for her? I have no idea. He didn't seem like he was afraid of anything or upset in that kind of way. It was more that he seemed all business. Like he just wanted to get checked in and to the bungalow and that was that."

"Maybe it was a long trip. Maybe he was tired. Where did they come from?"

Amanda still had their reservation up on the computer screen in front of her. "Los Angeles. So, yes, it was a long trip. And then there's the time zone difference. You're right. He was probably just tired. And I'm probably making too much out of it."

"I don't know about that," Carissa said. "Your instincts about the guests have been pretty spot on. You read people very well. And I know how concerned you are that guests have a good time while they're here."

"Thanks." Amanda glanced toward the doors the Hestons had gone through. "I just like to know how to best meet their needs and give them the kind of amazing experience that I want Mother's to be known for."

"And now you want to do something to make him happy, don't you."

"I can't help it but I do. And I don't have a clue what that is."

"I'm sure something will come to you, but this might be a case where doing nothing is exactly what he needs. Sometimes being left alone is the reason people come here."

"I know, you're right. And he did mention that." But Amanda couldn't get Conrad off her mind. If he didn't enjoy his stay here, he might leave a bad review for the resort, which wouldn't be great, but the resort would recover.

What was worse was that he might feel like he'd wasted money by coming here. A stay at Mother's was very expensive. It was part of why she bent over backwards to make guests happy.

She needed to do some more digging on Conrad to see if she could find something he really enjoyed. Maybe a certain kind of drink or a special meal or a favorite dessert. Maybe even a particular new book that he was looking forward to reading. Thanks to Katie and her publishing connections, Amanda might be able to get a thing like that for him before anyone else had it.

Of course, she was just guessing. She had no idea what might make him happy.

But, as she returned to her office behind the registration desk, she was determined to find out.

Chapter Two

*O*livia smiled at the report she'd just run. The results weren't any big surprise. She was too on top of things for that to happen. But it was so nice to see those numbers in black and white. To see the proof of what she knew was happening. That was, of course, that the second phase of Mother's, opened just a few months ago, was a resounding success.

The family bungalows—an addition they'd all been concerned about, since children hadn't been previously welcomed to Mother's—were hugely popular. The bookings, which extended nearly six months out now, were proof of that.

It wasn't just families that were coming to Mother's now, though. As Olivia dug into the demographics of their guests, it was easy to see that the family bungalows had broader appeal. They'd started getting groups, often of younger people, but not always.

In fact, one of the family bungalows was

currently occupied by three older women, all friends, who'd wanted to get away together.

Olivia loved that idea of a girls' vacation. Friendships like that were worth their weight in gold. She knew from firsthand experience.

In addition to the new bungalows, the two new eateries, both the fast-casual Castaways and the more upscale Iris's, were doing great. Castaways, which featured later hours and a brand-new pizza oven, was a huge hit, due in great part to the pizzas.

Olivia had recently spoken to Grace and her husband, head chef David, about the possibility of adding a second pizza oven on that side of things.

Pizza, it seemed, was a very popular item to order poolside. Olivia could understand that. It was something that most people didn't mind eating even if it got cold, and it was easy to eat. No utensils required.

It helped that David, along with some of his cooks and the new pizza maker, Jamarcus, had come up with some really incredible flavor combinations and not only the traditional ones. They were even making dessert pizzas, things like Nutella with bananas and strawberries and a s'mores pizza that was downright sinful.

Olivia had tried a slice of that for herself, which

was how she knew. Even though she was still eating healthy and swimming laps, she allowed herself the occasional indulgence. Hard not to when surrounded by such tempting things all the time.

She began writing up her notes on the report, turning it into something more easily understood, so she could send it out to the owners' email loop. She was excited to share the information with the girls and Iris. Numbers didn't lie and these showed just how well their hard work had paid off.

She spent another half an hour finalizing the report, then writing the email that would go along with it, proofing both, then proofing them once more.

Finally happy with how it all looked, she hit Send. She had one more item on her to-do list, and that was to get a start on payroll.

Two hours later, she'd gone through all of the timesheets to make sure she had the right number of hours each hourly employee had worked. The salaried employees, of which she was one, as were the four women she co-owned the resort and island with, were much easier. Some of the other salaried employees were Chef David and Captain Eddie, the man who'd captured Olivia's heart since she'd come to the island.

She smiled thinking about him, and kept smiling as she changed the date for the billing period, checked a box to approve the amounts, then hit Pay Now. All of them had their money directly deposited into their accounts.

Most of the employees did, actually. Including Eddie, who'd recently gotten a raise, something that had been well-deserved. The increase in his pay had nothing to do with her being madly in love with him. If it had, he would have gotten the raise months ago.

She glanced at her watch. He wore a nearly identical one, the men's version, because unbeknownst to them, they'd gotten the same nautical watch for each other for Christmas. She couldn't help but think of him every time she looked at the time.

And she already thought of him quite a lot.

They were going out on the boat tonight. The boat she'd just bought. It wasn't as fancy as the pontoon that Owen had given Katie as a Christmas present, but Olivia was thrilled with it. The second-hand cruiser had a small cabin, large enough to stay overnight in. It also had plenty of comfortable seating and a bimini top for shade. She loved everything about it and she was especially grateful to

Eddie, who'd done all the hard work of finding the boat and making sure it was in good condition.

But she'd done all the negotiating. When it came to numbers, there was no one who could compete with her.

Eddie had helped her pick the boat up yesterday and tonight would be its real maiden voyage. She was definitely looking forward to it. She looked forward to any evening spent with Eddie, which was most of them.

Although lately, they hadn't been seeing quite as much of each other, because of her daughter's upcoming wedding. Olivia had been trying to help Jenny where she could. Amanda, who'd been a wedding planner and currently handled all of the weddings on the island, had offered to help as a gift, but Jenny felt that was too much to ask. She'd been doing it all herself so far.

Olivia wasn't sure how that was going. Jenny always just said everything was fine, but Olivia had her doubts.

In less than two weeks, Jenny and Nick would be tying the knot in a beautiful beach ceremony. Katie and Owen were also getting married just three days from now, but all Olivia had to do for that was show up.

Jenny's wedding required a good deal of input but only when Jenny asked. Olivia wasn't about to push her ideas onto her daughter. Jenny was a very capable adult and since she wanted to plan and organize her own wedding, Olivia was letting her. Jenny had said right away that she welcomed her mother's help and Olivia was happy to be included. Whatever Jenny needed, she did.

The only part she wasn't happy about was Jenny including her father in the ceremony, but Olivia had kept that to herself. It was understandable that Jenny would want her dad there.

Olivia blew out a breath. Her ex-husband, Simon, would be arriving on the island the day before the wedding. She wasn't exactly looking forward to seeing him, but according to Jenny, he'd been sober for a while.

She hoped that was true. And that it remained true once he got here. Drunk Simon wasn't fit for any event, let alone their only child's wedding.

Being married to Simon hadn't been easy. At times, it had been downright awful. She had no desire to think about any of that, but it was hard not to with his impending visit looming ever closer.

She needed time with Eddie more than ever. He

was such a good reminder of how far she'd come, and how different – and joyous – her life was now.

At five o'clock, she saved her work, turned off her computer, and locked her office. The walk back to her bungalow in the staff area of the island was always something she looked forward to. It gave her a chance to see how guests were enjoying everything and to have a look around the property.

It wasn't often she found anything amiss. They'd recently added two new groundskeepers to the crew to help with the expansion of the resort and the employees as a whole excelled at keeping things in pristine condition.

There was occasionally the errant bit of trash left by a careless guest, though. Olivia didn't mind picking that up, though it bothered her that guests weren't a little more aware of their surroundings. But then, some of them *expected* to be picked up after. Probably used to a houseful of staff that did it for them. The wealthy were just a different breed. Except for Owen. He was pretty normal, for a billionaire.

Iris, who was technically only a millionaire, was a little eccentric, and only in the best possible way. Iris was a saint, in Olivia's book. She was pretty sure the rest of the women felt that way, too. After all, Iris, the woman who'd been their house mother when they'd all been in the Delta Sig sorority, was the reason they were here. The reason they were part-owners of this magnificent place.

Olivia touched the diamond pendant on the chain around her neck as she took the path that led to the staff area. That diamond had been a gift from Iris for Christmas. All the women had gotten one, as if she hadn't already given them enough with the island and the resort.

Olivia felt like she lived in a constant state of bliss these days and knowing that she was about to see Eddie lifted her spirits even higher.

But as she followed the path around to her bungalow, she saw Jenny sitting on the steps of her front porch.

Jenny got up as Olivia approached. Her furrowed brow and tight jaw made it clear she was unhappy. "Mom, I've been trying to reach you. Where have you been?"

"At the office." She pulled out her phone, which was on silent. Being interrupted while doing payroll seemed like an easy way to make a mistake. She saw she'd missed quite a few messages. "I'm sorry. What's wrong?"

Jenny let out a woebegone sigh. "Yolanda. Less

than two weeks from the wedding and Nick's mother is insisting I wear her wedding dress to get married in."

Olivia just stared at her daughter, stunned by the news. Nick and his mother had reconciled over Christmas, which was why Yolanda was here now, although she'd arrived for the wedding much earlier than anyone had expected. Olivia had guessed that despite the reconciliation, she remained a somewhat difficult woman with a lot of strange and superstitious beliefs. But this?

Olivia shook her head, her protective motherly instincts kicking in as she headed for her bungalow stairs. This was a bridge too far.

Chapter Three

$\mathcal{J}$enny had been trying not to break down since Yolanda arrived, but the wedding dress thing was just too much. She needed her mother in a way that defied logic. She felt like a kid again, running to her mom for help, but she didn't care. "Mom, what am I going to do?"

Olivia stomped up the steps, key in hand, and began to unlock the door. "Come inside and we'll figure something out. But obviously, you're *not* going to wear her dress. I can't even imagine what her dress looks like it."

"It's very...big. And blingy. And while I have nothing against sparkle, this thing has actual rhinestones on it that are bigger than my thumb. Plus, it looks like lingerie. And not in a good way."

Her mother's lip curled. "You mean she actually brought it with her?"

Jenny put her hands on her hips. "She came with four suitcases. Four. Yeah, she brought it."

Olivia sighed toward the sky. "That woman." She pursed her lips. "Your dress is beautiful and very you and perfect for a beach ceremony. There's no reason for her to suggest such a thing except that she's trying to take control."

"Or worse," Jenny said.

Her mother opened the door and stepped back to let Jenny go inside first. "What do you mean, worse?"

Jenny sighed, almost on the verge of tears. "I think...I think she might be trying to break Nick and I up."

"What?" Olivia shut the door so hard it almost slammed. "You're about to get married. I know it's not a big wedding, but things are in place. Flowers are ordered, the menu is set, the guests have been invited. Does she really think that's something she can accomplish?" She shook her head. "Forget I asked. Of course she does. She kept Nick away from Arthur until the poor man died."

A sob tore from Jenny's throat. "Mom, I love him. I can't lose him."

"He's not going to call things off because you don't want to wear his mother's dress, I promise you that, sweetheart. Nick's eyes were opened to Yolanda's shenanigans a long time ago. Not to mention he loves you very much. I can see it in his eyes every time he looks at you."

Hearing her mom say that helped a lot. Jenny exhaled, but the breath came out shuddery and tears still felt imminent. She couldn't help it. The whole thing had nearly pushed her to her breaking point. "It's not just the dress. It's...everything. She criticized the menu, saying the food choices are boring and that Nick is used to more interesting cuisine, since he's lived in so many countries and didn't I care about that. Then she said my color choices of aqua and gold are overdone and asked me why I picked them. I mean, it's a *beach* wedding. How is aqua not right? And she keeps saying how it's a good thing she came when she did."

"She's awful," Olivia said. "Your colors are perfect. So is your menu. Nick helped you decide on it!"

"I know, but wait—there's more." Jenny held up her hand to tick things off on her fingers. "My guest list is too small. Apparently, we should have allowed her to invite some of her friends. And by some, I mean at least twenty. My flowers look cheap. Well, she said they look like we're on a budget, which we are. It's ridiculous to spend a ton of money on a wedding when that money could be put toward our lives together."

"Agreed," Olivia said with a proud nod.

Jenny knew her mother would agree with that one. If there was anything she'd learned from her mom, it was the importance of weighing a purchase in the present against the value of an investment for the future. She tapped another finger. "She asked if that budget was the reason we were going with a DJ instead of live music. Nick told her yes, but it's also so we can play a variety of songs. She rolled her eyes. She's also offered suggestions on how to do my hair, what my makeup should look like, what kind of jewelry I should wear, and told me several times that flipflops are not appropriate attire for a bride."

"For a beach wedding? I strongly disagree. Those flipflops you got with the little pearls on them are completely bridal. And honestly, it's yours and Nick's day. If you both wanted to go barefoot, that would be entirely up to you."

"Trust me, I've thought about it." Jenny clenched her hands into fists. "Mom, she's making me crazy."

"Sweetheart, that is probably her plan."

"Yeah, you're right. I'm sure it is." Jenny was just

afraid that Yolanda's plan might be working. It was certainly wearing her down.

Olivia put her arm around Jenny. "Yolanda also has to know that at this late stage, none of those things can be changed."

Jenny nodded. "She's been married enough times. She should know."

Olivia snorted before going into the kitchen. "Good point. You want something to drink? Water? Tea? Coffee? I can make a pot."

"No, I'm fine. And I don't want any caffeine. I need to be able to sleep tonight." Jenny took a seat at the kitchen counter. "I've been doing my best to be civil. More than that, really. I've been trying to act like I'm listening and taking in her suggestions and that she isn't a complete lunatic, but it's getting harder and harder."

"I bet." Her mom filled a glass with ice and water. "Do you want me to talk to her? Mother to mother?"

Jenny straightened and shook her head. "No. I mean, I would love that, and I appreciate the offer, but then she'd just know she was getting to me. And I really don't want her to feel like she's got the upper hand. Know what I mean?"

"I do. But you're already under enough stress.

You don't need her nonsense on top of all the normal wedding stuff."

"You don't even know how right you are." Jenny rolled her shoulders. She loved her PR job and she was happy to have it, but sometimes it would be nice to have an assistant. Which was silly, because this was probably the only time she'd think that and she was never getting married again. "Owen's got me engaged in a deliberate misinformation campaign for him."

Olivia's brows bent. "Meaning...?"

"Meaning I've been spending the last couple of weeks filling his and Katie's social media with misleading information. Nothing bad. It's just a way of keeping the press from thinking there's any chance they're getting married this week. Like, for example, I just posted for him today about an upcoming meeting and how productive travel can be along with a picture of a book on a seat that looks like it could be in his jet."

Olivia nodded. "That's really smart. I know he and Katie are concerned that the paparazzi are going to ruin it."

"I can't blame the press for wanting pictures, though."

Olivia snorted. "I can. They should leave people alone."

"Mom, this is Owen Monk we're talking about. Tech billionaire. Launcher of the OM coin, which somehow made cryptocurrency a bigger deal than it already was. Owner of Orion's Belt, the satellite company that is making internet access free and available in Third World countries."

"I'm very aware of Owen's achievements."

"And then there's Katie, who basically blew up the web on her own last year with all the pen name stuff and the business about her giving up her baby for adoption."

Olivia nodded. "I know."

"The two of them are still big news. It's kind of crazy the requests I've been getting. People are trying to get to both of them through me. Especially Owen. They know I do his PR now and my inbox is full every day with people wanting to meet him, show him their ideas, or just set up an interview with him. It's nuts."

Olivia's brows lifted. "I had no idea."

Jenny nodded. "I get some for Katie, too, but not the volume I do for him."

"No wonder you're so stressed."

Jenny took a breath. It was really good to tell her

mom all of this. Just saying it all out loud made her feel better. "I'll be all right."

"You're sure?"

"Yeah." Jenny rubbed the back of her neck. "Just so long as Yolanda doesn't talk Nick into canceling the wedding."

Chapter Four

Katie twirled once before the mirror, catching her sister's gaze in the reflection. "It's just the most beautiful dress I've ever owned. It's a shame I only get to wear it for one day."

"I know," Sophie said. She was sitting on the bed behind Katie, her legs crossed. "Maybe there's something you could do to it to make it wearable again. Like getting it dyed? Or cutting it shorter? Or both?"

"Maybe." Katie nodded as she admired the gown. It was a simple, floor-length halter-neck silhouette, but the dress was covered in icy crystals, delicate beading, lace appliqués, and handmade ribbon flowers. It was slightly bohemian and utterly romantic.

She planned to wear a crown of white and pale pink roses accented by a little baby's breath, ribbon, and a few crystals for sparkle.

She turned to face Sophie as a sudden fear struck her. "Tell me the truth. Do I look ridiculous in this? Is it too young for me?"

Sophie shook her head and laughed. "No to either of those things. Would you stop worrying about that? Katie, you have *never* been married. You have earned the right to wear whatever you want on your special day. Does the dress make you happy?"

Katie smiled. "It really does. And I know you're going to say that's all that matters."

"Because it's true. Owen's going to love it, too."

Katie turned back to the mirror. "I hope so."

"You could get married in a garbage bag and he'd still think you were beautiful."

Katie laughed. "I don't know about that."

"I do. He's more in love with you than any hero of any book you've ever written has been in love with the heroine."

Katie's grin widened and her heart felt full. Her sister's words rang true. Owen loved her more than she'd ever been loved before. More than she'd thought it possible to be loved. She sighed out of pure happiness. "The feeling's mutual."

"Put the veil on."

The veil was just a waist-length bit of tulle, edged in crystals. It would sit right below the flower crown attached to Katie's hair with two clips. "I'm not sure I can get it to stay without my hair being done."

She took it out of the box and placed it approximately where she thought it would sit. It wasn't secure but it was good enough for a trial run. "What do you think?"

Sophie looked a little misty-eyed. "You look so beautiful. You two are going to be the best-looking couple to ever get married."

"I think that title will probably belong to Jenny and Nick, but I appreciate you saying it all the same. I can't wait to see Owen in his suit." He'd asked her what he should wear and she'd suggested ivory linen, so he'd gone right out and had a suit made.

He was pairing the suit with a white shirt and a pale pink tie to match the roses in her crown and bouquet.

"It's going to be an amazing wedding. Are you sure it's going to be paparazzi-free?"

"No, I'm not," Katie said. "But Owen and Gage are doing everything they can to make that happen."

Owen was a sitting target here on Compass Key. The paps knew where he lived and since he and Katie had become an item, the paparazzi loved photographing them together. They'd wreaked havoc on Katie's life when they'd not only outed her as the woman behind the Iris Deveraux pen name, but revealed that she'd given up a child for adoption when she'd been much younger.

But Owen and Gage, his head of security, had

assured her they had a plan for the wedding that would ensure it was private, a real friends-and-family-only affair.

She hoped that was true. She'd had enough of the paparazzi since they'd shared her life with the world.

Although, it hadn't all been bad. The child she'd given up had found her and they'd reconnected, building a relationship she never thought she'd have.

That child, now a grown man with a wife and children of his own, was due in the day before the wedding. "I'm so glad we were able to do the wedding over spring break so Josh and Christy and the kids can be here."

"Me, too," Sophie said. "I can't wait to see Dakota and Gunner. I love those babies so much."

"Same here. And Dakota is going to make the most adorable flower girl."

"Agreed." Sophie grinned. "But I'm pretty excited to see Uncle Hutch, too."

Katie pressed her hands together. "Oh, so am I. It's been too long." Their late mother's eldest brother, Emerson Hutch, was arriving late this evening. He was a complete character and they both loved him dearly. At seventy-nine, Uncle Hutch was still a working musician, living in New Orleans, where he played piano with a jazz band and did a few nights as a solo act, as well.

Katie was thrilled that he'd not only agreed to come but was going to do her the honor of walking her down the aisle. Wherever that aisle might be. Owen still hadn't told her where they were getting married, just that he'd secured a venue that would keep them safe from prying eyes.

Sophie sat back as Fabio, Katie's cat, jumped up onto the bed and meowed for attention. Sophie hugged him and kissed his head. "I'm going to miss this guy so much."

Katie gave her a look. "I'm only moving five minutes away. By bike."

"I know," Sophie said, her gaze growing wistful. "But it's going to be weird. We've lived together pretty much our entire adult lives. And now...that's coming to an end."

Katie nodded. "It makes me a little sad. But we'll still be close." Last year, Owen had paid for a boardwalk to be built connecting the two ends of Compass Key. Basically, his property and Iris's house, where Katie and Sophie occupied the middle floor of the three-story residence.

Sophie's smile didn't quite reach her eyes. "We will. But it won't be the same."

That was true. Katie knew it. She went a little closer to her sister. "Why don't you take Owen up on his offer and move into the guest house?"

Sophie scratched Fabio behind the ears. "No, I can't do that. It'll freak Gage out. He's already gotten a little...odd lately. I'm sure it's all this wedding business. I think he *thinks* I'm going to start pressuring him to propose. I'm not, though. I'm really happy with how things are. Or were."

Katie would have loved to say that wasn't true, but she'd seen it for herself. Whenever she and Owen were discussing the wedding plans, Gage seemed to get a distant look in his eyes. Like he was trying to shut it all out.

Sophie sighed. "No, moving into the guest house would only make it seem like I was desperate to be closer to him."

"Why don't you just talk to him about it? Stop pretending there's no elephant in the room and just have the discussion?"

Sophie hugged Fabio tight. "Because I'm afraid it won't go well and he'll end up breaking up with me. I really like him, Katie. No, that's wrong. I love him.

I'd much rather be with him, unmarried, than be without him."

Katie hiked up her dress a few inches and sat on the bed next to her sister. "I still think you should talk to him. He loves you. I know he does. He's not going to bolt just because you want to talk about your future."

Sophie cocked an eyebrow, clearly skeptical. "Sure. Because no man has ever in his life freaked out about having a relationship talk."

"Okay, I know it's a possibility. But I don't think Gage is that guy." Gage was former military, and maybe not the biggest conversationalist, and also a tiny bit hard to read sometimes, but he was a *really* good guy. Owen wouldn't have hired him otherwise. "Could there be something else going on?"

"Like what?"

Katie didn't have an answer for that and she really wanted to help Sophie get through this. Was it possible that Gage didn't want to get that serious with Sophie? Katie honestly would have thought otherwise, with the way the two of them had been keeping company these last few months. "Do you want me to see if he's said anything to Owen? They are close. Maybe it's come up."

Sophie chewed on her bottom lip. "Yeah, maybe.

But be subtle about it. And make sure Owen doesn't say anything to Gage about you talking to him about me."

Katie almost smiled at her sister's dilemma but that wouldn't have helped, because she knew Sophie wouldn't see the humor in it. "I won't. And I'll make him promise not to say a word."

"Thanks. When are you going to see him?"

Katie glanced at the time. "Not until tomorrow. After all, we have Uncle Hutch coming in and I have a trial run at the salon for my hair today, which is what got me back into my dress. I had to see it on again."

Sophie snorted. "Please. You've put that dress on every day since it arrived."

"That's not true."

Sophie cut her eyes at her sister.

Katie laughed, because she knew her sister was right. She *had* put the dress on every day since it had arrived. "Okay, you're right, I have. But can you blame me?"

Sophie shook her head, a wry, slightly envious smile curving her mouth. "Not one single bit."

Chapter Five

"*D*on't forget to breathe. Breathing is important." The man Leigh Ann was stretching out on the mat was none other than Paul De Luca, easily one of the most famous men she'd ever met. Or put her hands on.

And he was here because of her.

"Right. Totally down with breathing." He nodded and exhaled, his forehead beaded with sweat from the workout she'd just put him through.

It was probably more truthful to say that he was here because of another celebrity, Rita Harlow, who had recommended Leigh Ann to Paul. Rita had come to Mother's as part of a personal rejuvenation experience that had included getting some work done, a brand-new diet, and training with Leigh Ann.

Unlike Rita, Paul wasn't exactly looking to rejuvenate himself. Men didn't face quite the same pressures in Hollywood that women did. They could get away with a touch of gray and a few character-building wrinkles.

But he did have thirty pounds to lose and at least ten to twelve pounds of muscle to gain for an upcoming role that he was obviously hoping would set his career on a new path.

Paul had been known as a funny guy for as long as he'd been in Hollywood. But, as he'd explained to Leigh Ann, he wanted to break free of that mold and do some serious acting. He'd caught a break with a new director and won a part as a retired boxer about to step back into the ring to gain the respect of his estranged son.

It sounded like the kind of movie that might even earn him an Oscar nod.

In the very early stages of training, Paul had decided he didn't want to subject himself to some L.A. meathead who'd put him through rigorous, bootcamp-style training to get him into shape, probably starving him on green smoothies at the same time.

Instead, he'd opted to start with a kinder, gentler approach that would help him lose the weight and get into the kind of shape that would allow him to withstand the boxing training he would still have to go through.

Leigh Ann and Mother's Resort was that kinder, gentler approach. He was three days in and had already been put on a fat-burning, muscle-building body recomposition meal plan by Kendall, the holistic nutritionist. Leigh Ann had started him on an intensive heavy weight program of lifting, along with some yoga to keep him limber and balanced, and plenty of stretching.

To help with healing and recovery, he was getting regular massages in the spa and taking advantage of the hot tub at his bungalow.

She finished counting out the hold for the stretch, then sat back. "That's it for today. I'm sure you're happy about that. How are you feeling?"

With a groan, he sat up. "Sore. But I'm dealing with it."

"That's to be expected. Your body is going through a real shakeup right now."

He nodded. "I know. And I'm not complaining." He grinned, his trademark megawatt smile lighting up the training room. "Not much, anyway."

She laughed. "A couple more days and the worst will be over, I promise."

"I can handle it. I'm already down six pounds."

She rolled her eyes good-naturedly. "Men have it so easy."

"It's true, we do, but it doesn't feel easy right now."

"No, I'm sure it doesn't. And you've been doing really well. You should be proud of yourself." She got to her feet as he did the same.

"I am. But I'm grateful for the help you and Kendall have been giving me, too. This place is fantastic. I can almost forget about the work I'm putting in when I stare out at that water. I'm so glad Rita recommended it."

So was Leigh Ann. Guests like Paul and Rita were exactly the kind Mother's needed. The kind with money, who didn't mind paying for extra services. And who would talk it up to their friends when they got home. "Are you off for a massage now?"

He snorted. "I'm going to soak in the hot tub until I feel like I can walk without looking like a ninety-year-old man, then I'm going to dinner." He patted his stomach. "At least that's one thing I don't have to suffer through. I never thought I'd be eating so much steak."

She smiled. "Got to keep that protein up."

"Hey, would you be interested in joining me? For dinner? I don't know if that's allowed but I'd love to talk about training some more and what's coming up next. Although you're probably tired of talking about that."

She shook her head. "I never get tired of talking about fitness." Not exactly the truth but what kind of a trainer would she be if she admitted otherwise? "And I appreciate the invite, but I have plans this evening."

She almost said "with my boyfriend," but that suddenly sounded so...high school. Like she needed Paul to know she was already taken. All he wanted was to talk about his training. It wasn't like he'd asked her to go for a romantic walk on the beach. Paul could have any woman he wanted. Leigh Ann was pretty sure she wouldn't even make the list.

He held his hands up. "Totally get it. I'll see you tomorrow then."

"Bright and early." Tomorrow was yoga and stretching in the morning, followed by two hours of weights in the afternoon.

With a wave, he draped his towel around his neck and headed out.

She watched after him for a second. She could already see the subtle changes in his face. His cheekbones were coming out a little more. The camera would love that.

She grabbed her bag, locked up the private training room, then did a quick walk-through to make sure the gym was in good order. After that, she'd head to the spa. She didn't need to go by there today, but she knew Katie was in the salon testing out her wedding hair and Leigh Ann wanted to see how things were going.

The salon fell under her management, so she wanted to be sure that Katie was happy and getting what she wanted. Of course, Katie wasn't a guest, she was an owner, so there was no reason to think the women at the salon wouldn't be doing everything in their power to make her happy. But Leigh Ann still wanted to stop by and see for herself.

She caught sight of herself in one of the mirrors as she headed for the doors. She was seeing Grant for dinner at her place this evening. Maybe she should get something done with her own hair. A wash and blowout, maybe?

She'd see if anyone had the time. Being around celebrities made her aware of just how much time, effort, and money they put into making themselves beautiful. It was hard not to want a little of that for herself.

She smoothed a finger over the skin between her brows. The spa now offered Botox and some fillers. Dr. Nick had found them a licensed physician's assistant who was skilled in that area and able to do those kinds of injections.

Leigh Ann had been thinking about trying some Botox. She sighed. It was hard not to be a little vain when you worked in the industry she did. Didn't help that she was surrounded by people who could afford to take care of themselves in whatever way they wanted.

Although she wasn't exactly poor.

Still looking into the mirror, she frowned, then smiled and scrunched up her nose, making her forehead wrinkle.

Why not give some of those things a try? Now that they offered the services at the spa, she should experience what they were like. At least once.

She walked out of the gym. She'd talk to Manuela, the head esthetician, when she got to the spa and see what she thought. Leigh Ann and Manuela had become pretty good friends and she trusted the woman to tell her the truth.

As Leigh Ann followed the path to the spa, she wondered what Grant would think. He might not like it. After all, she was his muse and if she did anything to change her appearance, it might bother him.

She didn't want to upset him, but she didn't want to let a man dictate what she did or didn't do, either.

She'd had enough of that with her ex-husband.

But Grant was not Marty. He was about as much not-Marty as a man could be. Grant always wanted her to be happy and if Botox was what might make her happy, he'd probably support it.

She exhaled, giving herself the same advice she'd just given Paul. She needed to breathe. More importantly, she needed to do her research first.

As the head of the spa and fitness center, it wouldn't hurt her to look as good as she possibly could.

She pushed through the spa doors and went up to the reception desk. What she needed was to talk to Manuela.

Chapter Six

*A*s Grace headed toward Castaways, she inhaled the smell of woodsmoke, yeasty dough, bubbling cheese, and garden-fresh tomato sauce. Probably what heaven smelled like, she thought. The guests seemed to agree. The new pizzas were a huge hit, which pleased her to no end, because anything that was good for the restaurants was good for business, and in turn, that was good for her and David.

They'd hired so many people and were banking on these two eateries to support all of that growth. So far, everything was going better than expected. Olivia's recently emailed report proved that.

Of course, it was still early days. It was possible that the guests would get bored with pizza. Although she doubted it. Not with the responses they'd been getting.

Even more amazing was how well things were going with being open to the non-guests. Granted, that was happening in a pretty limited way. They only allowed a certain number of outside guests and only on Fridays and Saturdays, the two nights most resort guests chose to go to the mainland for a meal. Outside guests also had to have a reservation and were given a wristband denoting them as a visitor.

So far, they'd had a mayor and a senator, which probably impressed Grace more than it did anyone else. She loved celebrities.

Castaways was hopping when she went in. Not unusual, even as the night wore on. Castaways was open late, another of the new things they were trying. Again, the longer hours had been well received.

Surprisingly, not just by the younger crowd that Mother's was starting to draw. David liked to stop in when he was done for the night and had told her repeatedly how guests of all ages seemed to like a late-night pizza snack.

Curtis Macarthur, the man they'd hired to oversee the two new eateries, gave her a wave. "Hey. How's it going?"

"Good. I was just about to ask you the same thing." Grace hadn't been completely sure about hiring Curt, because of their history as college sweethearts. He'd broken her heart by proposing, then disappearing, but they'd worked all of that out.

Curt was a different person now. And honestly, so was Grace.

"We're having a good night. Jamarcus came up with tonight's specialty pizza, Conch Alfredo, and it's been very popular. In fact, we probably have enough left to make two or three more and then it's eighty-sixed."

That meant it would no longer be available, because they'd run out of whatever they needed to make it. "Conch Alfredo? What's on it?"

"Bits of conch, diced roasted red pepper, and bacon pieces on a base of alfredo sauce topped with parm and fontina."

"Okay, that does sound good."

Curtis shook his head like he couldn't believe how well it was doing. "We're going to run it again a few more nights, see if the response stays the same and, if so, we'll probably add it to the menu."

"David's going to want to taste it. I do, too, honestly."

"Have you eaten? If not, I'll get Jamarcus to make you one."

"I haven't. That would be great. I'll take it over to The Palms to share with David."

"I'll get right on it."

David might be busy at The Palms, but he could

find the time to have a couple bites of the pizza. The resort's original restaurant had undergone a beautiful renovation that included a small expansion and a lot of glamour in the new décor. Grass cloth walls, marble floors, burnished gold and glass palm leaf dividers, all with touches of ivory, emerald green, and more gold, had made the space a real show-stopper.

And thanks to David, the food lived up to the experience. Chantelle, the pastry chef, now had two more working under her as they turned out incredible desserts for all three locations.

The signature dessert at Iris's was the key lime cake. At Castaways, it was something called a dark chocolate coconut bomb that reminded Grace of an elevated Mounds candy bar, and at The Palms, it was gold leaf-flecked chocolate torte with hints of passion fruit.

On an almost daily basis, Grace was awed by the plates coming out of the kitchens.

She settled in at one of the seats around the pizza bar, specifically designed so that guests could sit and watch the pizzas being made while eating there.

Jamarcus gave her a big smile. "Hi, Miss Grace."

He threw a circle of dough into the air, partly to stretch it out for the next pizza, but also for the show of it. Guests loved it. And Jamarcus loved to get them smiling, especially the kids.

"I hear your pizza special is a big hit."

He shrugged, his smile going a little shy. "You never know when something might click, you know?"

"I do know. I can't wait to try it. I'm going to take it over to The Palms with me."

His brows went up. "Chef David's going to try this?"

She nodded. "He is."

"All right. This is going to be my best one yet."

"Jamarcus, all of your pizzas are great."

"Thanks." His grin got bigger. "Say, Miss Grace. You know anything about Carissa? She works at the front desk."

"Depends. What are you trying to find out?"

"If she's single."

"Is that right?" Grace chuckled.

He nodded while he dressed the pizza. "She's pretty cute. Thought I might take a shot, you know?"

"Absolutely." They'd make a cute couple. "I'll see what I can find out."

"Thanks." He turned to put the pizza into the oven.

While she waited for it to cook, she studied the faces around her, listening in on some of the conversations of the people who seemed to be talking about the food. They were all happy, all enjoying their meals.

Castaways was designed to be more casual, and that message had been clearly received. There were a lot of guests in swimwear and coverups, but considering that a very fun pool was the centerpiece of this expansion, that was to be expected.

Over the calypso music playing inside the building, Grace could just hear the happy shrieks and laughter of children and parents playing outside. The Fun Pool had come by that nickname pretty quickly. With its lazy river, spray jets, grottos, slides, and shallow play area, the new aquatic area was really something special. About as different as night and day from the main pool, which had been designated as an adults-only area, but it served the new family demographic very well.

A family came to sit in the three remaining seats at the pizza bar. A mom, dad, and a little boy about four or five, Grace guessed.

He was in swim trunks and a T-shirt, both decorated with dinosaurs. Grace smiled and leaned forward to see him better. "Did you just come from the pool? Or are you going after dinner?"

"Both," he proudly announced.

His parents smiled. The dad answered, "All he wants to do is be in that pool." He ruffled his son's hair. "Can't say that I blame him. We don't get to swim very much in Wisconsin."

"I bet you don't."

Jamarcus took their order: A chicken barbeque pizza for the parents and a kids cheese and pepperoni for the little boy.

The mom leaned to see Grace. "Where are you from?"

Grace smiled. "Compass Key. I live here."

Her brows shot up. "You live here?"

Jamarcus laughed as he made their orders. "Y'all talking to Miss Grace. One of the owners of this whole place."

Both the parents blinked. The husband said, "Is that right?"

"It is," Grace said. "My husband, David, is the head chef, and I manage the back of the house as well as help plan special events. We live right here on the island."

The wife shook her head. "I can't imagine what it

must be like to live here. This place seems like paradise."

Grace could only nod and smile. "That's because it is."

Chapter Seven

*I*ris sat in her favorite spot: The side porch of her house. From her usual chair, she watched the sky change colors as the sun set. A soft, fragrant breeze drifted past, bringing the tang of salt, the sweetness of evening blooms, and the faintest hint of wood smoke.

It was a combination of scents she'd come to enjoy very much.

Even Calico Jack, currently curled up on her lap, seemed to like it. He'd occasionally lift his head when the breeze swept over them, nostrils flaring as he took in the aromas.

"What do you think, my friend? Do you like that? That smoke is from the pizza oven. You'd probably like pizza." She laughed softly as she ran her hand down his head and back, loving the softness of his fur and the subtle vibration of his purring.

His two companions, Mary Read and Anne Bonny, were sprawled on the nearby couch.

Normally, Iris would stare out at the water and

think about how good her life was. And her life *was* good. It was amazing.

But her normal peace and quiet had been slightly...marred by the somewhat unexpectedly early arrival of Yolanda Oscott, Nick's mother.

Her arrival *had* been expected, but not until next week. Instead, Yolanda had shown up almost a week and a half early, claiming she couldn't sit around at home and not help with the wedding.

In theory, that was a lovely gesture. In reality, Iris feared that Yolanda's help wasn't really help so much as it was a hindrance.

Poor Nick and Jenny. Since the woman had arrived, Iris had, from her porch on the house's main level, caught snippets of conversation on the third level between Yolanda and Nick, Yolanda and Jenny, and Nick and Jenny. Enough to understand that things were a little rocky since Yolanda had decided to help. At worst, she feared Jenny might call the whole thing off in frustration.

And even though Iris felt for the young people, she also didn't think it was her place to butt in. If Jenny needed help, she could reach out to her mother. Olivia would do whatever needed to be done. And Yolanda was Nick's mother, after all. If someone was going to set her straight, that duty fell to him.

Of course, Nick's father was Arthur Cotton, Iris's beloved late husband, but because of Yolanda's machinations, Iris had only just gotten to know Nick this past year.

Yolanda had done a marvelous job of keeping Nick and his father separated, sadly. Nick had grown up to realize what his mother had done, and made the decision to change his life accordingly. He'd arrived at Compass Key too late to meet his father, but Iris had welcomed him all the same, knowing it was what Arthur would have wanted.

Nick was a lovely young man, and a doctor to boot. Iris had been thrilled he'd decided to stay on. Then he and his mother had reconciled over Christmas, something Iris had fully supported. Family was very important. She wasn't going to stand in the way of Nick rebuilding his relationship with his mother.

Now, however, she was wondering about the wisdom of that reconciliation. Yolanda seemed to be playing power games once again. Games like that had no real winners.

Iris glanced at her ceiling, wondering what Yolanda was currently up to. The third floor had been quiet since Jenny had left earlier, headed toward her mother's bungalow. Perhaps calling in reinforcements?

If so, good for her. If Yolanda got in the way of those two young people getting married, Iris would have to step in. There was only so much she could take. She was sure Olivia and the rest of the girls would agree with her.

Vera came outside with a cup of tea and her Kindle. "Mind some company?"

"Happy to have it," Iris said.

Vera smiled at Calico Jack and then the cats on the couch. "Looks like you already have enough."

"There's always room for you, Vera." Iris couldn't imagine life without her housekeeper, who was really so much more. Caretaker, cook, and, most importantly, friend. "That was an excellent dinner. That grouper was spectacular."

"Thanks." Vera settled on the couch between Mary Read and Anne Bonny. "You want anything else?"

"I might have a cup of tea later, but I'm fine. You sit and relax."

Vera set her cup down, then put her feet up on the little table in front of the couch. "You don't have to tell me twice."

She opened up her Kindle, but lowered her voice to say something else. "Anything new upstairs?"

Iris knew exactly what she meant. "Nothing. Been quiet since Jenny left."

"Hmm."

Iris nodded. "I know."

Vera went back to reading and Iris wished she'd brought her own Kindle out with her. She looked down at Calico Jack, who showed no signs of moving. "My darling boy, I know you're comfortable, but you might have to move."

"Do you need something?" Vera asked.

"I was thinking I'd get my Kindle. You inspired me. Plus, that new Hope Holloway book I'm reading is just marvelous."

"Maybe I'll read that after this thriller." Vera put her ereader aside. "I'll get your Kindle for you. I'd hate to see poor Jack disturbed."

Iris chuckled. "It's a good thing he's not spoiled."

"I'll say." Vera got up. "On your nightstand?"

"Yes. Thank you so much."

Vera returned shortly, handing the device to Iris. "Here you go."

Movement down below caught Iris's attention. "Look. I think that's our Jenny coming back now. I'm sure she went to see Olivia."

Vera peered at the path from the staff quarters. "And I bet Olivia gave her some good advice. Namely, to ignore that woman."

"I hope so."

Vera went back to the couch. Iris opened the cover of her Kindle and swiped to bring it to life. A second later, it displayed the last page she'd been on.

As good as her book was, her attention was focused elsewhere. Upstairs. She was listening intently to see if she could catch any snippets of conversation. She supposed such eavesdropping made her a nosy old biddy, but she didn't care one bit.

Jenny and Nick were dear to her. Having such young, vibrant people so close made her feel younger. And even if Nick hadn't been Arthur's son, he'd saved her life. There was nothing she wouldn't do for him.

"You're not reading, are you," Vera said softly.

Iris gave a little shake of her head. "No. I can't help myself."

"Don't feel bad," Vera said. "I've been listening, too. I don't hear anything, though."

Iris sighed. "Maybe that's a good thing."

"You know," Vera began. "You could ask Nick to come see you. For a medical reason, I mean. It would be the perfect cover to talk to him. See how he thinks things are going."

Iris twisted slightly to see Vera better. "That's not a bad idea. But I'm as healthy as a horse. What medical reason could I have?"

Vera shrugged. "Tell him you're thinking about taking up a new exercise program. They always say to consult your doctor before starting a thing like that."

"True. What kind of exercise program?"

Vera laughed. "Badminton? I don't know. You'll think of something."

Iris snorted out a laugh. "Badminton? Have you been drinking? Where would I do that? It's got to be plausible."

"Okay, how about...tell him you're thinking about doing Pilates. That should do it."

"Isn't that the same thing as yoga?"

"No. Google it. It's a lot of core work and stretching, I think."

Iris nodded. "If I'm doing it, you are, too."

"It's just pretend," Vera said. "I get enough exercise taking care of this house."

Iris grinned. "I suppose you do. Good idea." She took her phone from her pocket and sent Nick a text.

She'd see for herself just how much influence Yolanda had over him.

If necessary, Iris would intervene. Maybe she'd never had the chance to act as Nick's stepmother when during her years with Arthur, but she considered Nick family all the same. And family was the greatest treasure there was. One worth protecting with all your might.

Chapter Eight

*a*manda wasn't sleepy but swaying gently in the hammock Duke had recently installed on his back deck was enough to lull anyone into a semiconscious state. Although having Duke next to her ought to be more than enough to keep her awake.

She was just so comfortable lying next to him, his arm around her, her head on his shoulder. Hard not to be totally relaxed like that. "I don't want this to ever end."

"It's not going to." He kissed the top of her head. "We're going to see to that next September."

She smiled. They'd agreed to a long engagement, in part because they were in no rush, but also to give her and her mother time to get on solid footing for the first time. *If* it was going to happen. Amanda still occasionally had her doubts. Militant Marge was a tough nut to crack. "Yes, we will."

"How was your day?"

"Good. Nothing too major. Couple of guests

checked out. And a couple of new guests came in. How was your day?"

"Installed a new condenser in the air conditioning unit on Bungalow 12. That was exciting."

She laughed, knowing there was nothing exciting about it at all. "I'm sure it was."

"No, really. I'm pretty sure the woman in that bungalow made me an indecent offer."

Now completely awake, Amanda put her hand on his chest and pushed up to see him. "What does that mean?"

"She offered me a beer from the mini-fridge and asked if I wanted to come inside to cool down. When I mentioned that the AC was temporarily disconnected because I was working on it, she said the shower was operating just fine."

Amanda's mouth fell open. "Seriously?"

He nodded, looking remarkably unaffected by the whole thing. "Yep."

"You act like it's no big deal. Like it happens all the time."

"Well, I wouldn't say *all* the time..."

She sucked in a breath and tried to sit up further, which was virtually impossible in a hammock. "Duke. How often does it happen?"

"A couple times a month? Maybe?"

She just stared at him and blinked. "I don't even know what to say. I realize you're a very attractive man with a great body but— Stop grinning like that."

He laughed. "Babe, it's no big thing. It's not like I'm going to act on any of the come-ons." He tugged her back down next to him. "I'm already spoken for."

"I know that, and you know that, but *they* don't know that."

"Trust me, I make it clear."

"How?" She settled in beside him again, but this was an answer she was eager to hear.

"For one thing, I play dumb. Like I don't have a clue what they're talking about. But then I usually work in a mention of my fiancée and that does the trick."

Amanda smiled despite being upset that a guest had hit on him. That was really inappropriate. "A mention how?"

"Today I told the woman in Bungalow 12 that I'd already showered at my fiancée's house and that I was good."

Amanda's laugh came out like a little bark. "Hah! Sorry for being jealous."

"Don't apologize. I like it. You look hot when you're all green-eyed. Hotter."

She laughed. "You're crazy."

He pulled her closer. "About you."

She sighed and drifted back into the blissful half-aware state she'd been in. The hammock swayed, and the breeze drifted over them like a gentle caress. The solar-powered torches Duke had added to his back deck flickered with astonishing realism, adding a little atmosphere to the already beautiful evening.

"Dinner was good," he said softly.

"Thanks." She'd made white bean chicken chili and served it with a crusty loaf of bread. It was interesting to her how much she enjoyed cooking these days, but then part of that was because Duke was so appreciative. It was nice to cook for someone who genuinely valued the effort you made. And complimented the food.

"How about tomorrow night I do some steaks on the grill?"

"Sounds good to me." Her mind went back to the Hestons, as it had been all day. "You ever have a feeling about something or someone? Like you know there's something off but you can't quite figure out what it is?"

"Sure," he said. "Often enough. My dad always says the more you listen to those instincts, the sharper they get. It's how you train yourself to key in on those feelings. You have one today?"

"I did. About a couple that checked in."

"What bothered you about them?"

"I don't know. They just seemed...not quite right. Not them, exactly. It was him, really. He seemed almost bothered to be here. Like it was an inconvenience. Not like something he was looking forward to. He didn't seem at all like a man on vacation at one of the most exclusive resorts in the world."

"Maybe that's exactly why he's here."

"Carissa said the same thing. And I know there are all sorts of reasons why he might be in that kind of mood, but..." She just shook her head.

"But that little thing inside you said it was more than that."

"Yes." She loved how well he understood her.

"You want me to visit their bungalow on a maintenance check? See if I can get a feel for them? Maybe there's something more going on."

She quickly shook her head. "I appreciate that but I don't think it's any of our business. Unless they make it our business. I just can't stop thinking about them. There was something that caught my eye about his watch, too. But again, I can't tell you what. It just seemed not quite right."

Duke loved watches. "What kind was it?"

"Pretty sure it was a Rolex Submariner. Possibly an older one? Again, not sure."

"Either way, nice piece. Worth a good bit, too."

"She had an expensive handbag, so it wasn't out of place for him to have a watch like that, but it still made me take a second look for a reason I can't name."

"You've gotten pretty good at knowing your high-end goods."

She laughed. "It's kind of a weird thing to be good at, but I do like taking the measure of the guests that way."

"But you don't know what it was about the watch?"

She shook her head. "I don't. I wish I could tell you." She thought about that a little more. "Maybe I'll look some Rolex Submariners up online tomorrow. That might help me figure it out."

"You're not going to be able to let this go, are you?"

She sighed. "I will. I promise. I'm not going to get obsessed. I just feel protective of this place and if something isn't right, especially if that something is a guest, it bothers me."

"I get it. It's what makes you so good at what you

do. Nothing wrong with that. If you want some help, just ask."

"Thanks." But she decided right then that she wasn't going to mention it again. She had a lot of other guests to take care of. If the Hestons needed something, they knew where the front desk was.

Chapter Nine

As the evening's cool air sailed past, Olivia's smile was so effortless it felt permanent. Driving the boat was just so much fun. Even more because the boat belonged to her. Didn't matter that she was going slow. Didn't matter that it was night. All that mattered was that she was in control of it. And that Eddie was by her side.

"So, Captain," he said. "How does it feel to be at the helm of your own craft?"

"It feels really good. Like I'm the boss. But also very free. I could take us anywhere right now."

"Just not back to Cuba."

She laughed. "No, not there. You did a great job finding this boat. I love it."

He stood next to her, his arm around her waist. "I enjoyed doing it. I've helped a lot of people find boats before, but never one I was also in love with."

She glanced over at him, giving him a quick peck on the cheek. "Thank you. For everything."

The running lights gleamed off the dark water

and, in the distance, another halo of light along the horizon outlined the mainland. Along the way, buoys marked the channels. She slowed even further, bringing the boat down to a crawl. "It's so beautiful out here at night. The air feels different and the stars are just so bright and clear."

He nodded. "I like being out at night. Or early morning. That's something we should do sometime. Watch the sunrise over the open water. It's so much bigger when you see it like that."

"Put it on the list."

They'd been making a list of things they wanted to do together.

"Done," Eddie said. He opened up the cooler. "You want a root beer?"

"I'd love one."

He got her a bottle and took the top off before handing it over. He lifted his. "To the *Sea Note*." She smiled at the name of her new vessel and they clinked their bottles together before taking a drink.

He gave her a curious look. "You haven't said much about the wedding and you've been talking about it nonstop for a while now. I don't know if that's good or bad."

Olivia sighed. "You're awfully perceptive."

"It's not good, is it?"

"It's...difficult." She settled into the driver's seat a little more.

He came to stand beside her. "Yolanda?"

She laughed but only because he'd guessed so well, not because it was funny. "Yes. She's driving Jenny crazy. Jenny came over to talk to me about it today. She was waiting on my front porch when I got home."

"That bad, huh?"

"Oh, worse than that. Jenny thinks, and I'm not so sure she's wrong, that Yolanda is trying to create enough waves that the wedding doesn't happen."

"*Ay caramba.*"

"Exactly." She explained what Jenny had told her, about all the things Yolanda had commented on that pertained to the wedding.

He frowned. "That woman is poison."

"I don't want to think that about her, but she's certainly not helping." Olivia blew air through her nostrils. "Maybe she doesn't realize what she's doing. Maybe she's so used to being critical, that's all she knows how to do. Or...maybe she knows exactly what she's doing and Jenny's right. I don't want that to be true."

"Neither do I," Eddie said. "But Jenny's very smart. And she understands people very well."

"You're right about that," Olivia said. "So what do I do? Because Jenny doesn't want me to say anything. She thinks that will just give Yolanda more fuel to keep doing what she's doing. That Yolanda will know she's gotten to Jenny if I step in."

He nodded slowly. "I can see that." He lifted his bottle for another drink.

"Yeah. Unfortunately, so can I. So what do I do?"

"You can let Jenny vent as much as she wants, and just be ready to intervene when she tells you it's okay to."

"I'm letting her vent, I promise. But I'm also worried about my child's mental health. She's working a full-time job in addition to planning this wedding. She seemed pretty stressed. I don't want her to get sick. Or have some kind of breakdown. Or do anything else that might impact the wedding. Because that would just mean Yolanda wins."

His brows lifted. "That bad, huh?"

She nodded and took a sip of her root beer. "Yes."

"Then you have to do something."

"I agree. But what can I do that will help without upsetting Jenny?"

"That's the tricky part."

"Isn't it, though." Olivia had already tried to think of a solution and come up short.

Eddie leaned back. "You know, a Cuban mother wouldn't have asked if she could speak to Yolanda. Just gone after her with a slipper."

Olivia laughed, happy for the break in the seriousness of the conversation. "Maybe I should try that. I don't think Yolanda could run away from me very fast in those high heels she wears."

"Nick has to know this is going on, right?"

"He does. Jenny told me enough to know that."

"Then it's kind of his place to speak to his mother. Jenny's about to be his wife. He needs to stand up for her."

"You think I should tell Nick that?" She wasn't sure she could. Confrontation wasn't her favorite thing. Although for Jenny, Olivia would do anything.

"Listen, Yolanda might be his mother, but you're about to be his mother-in-law. There's a certain power in that."

Olivia gave that some thought. "I guess so."

"What was your relationship like with your mother-in-law?"

She shook her head. "I didn't have one. My ex-husband's parents weren't in the picture. Personally, I think they were happy to foist him off on me."

"Oh." Eddie knew about her past with Simon, about his alcoholism and the difficulties it had created in their tempestuous marriage. "Well, I can tell you that with mine, as brief as that marriage was, I would have done pretty much whatever she told me to do. I was a little afraid of her."

"Maybe that's just a Cuban thing."

"Maybe, but I don't think so. And it's worth a shot."

"You're right. It is. Jenny said not to talk to Yolanda. She didn't say anything about not talking to Nick. But I can't just stroll into their place and say I need to talk to him. Jenny will know something's up. Yolanda, too."

"No, that's not the way to do it."

She looked at him. "Any suggestions?"

He grinned. "Sure. Make him come to you. To your office. But don't tell him why he's been called in. Just let the reason why marinate in his head. You're the CFO. He'll think it's got something to do with money. By the time he arrives and you give him the real reason, he'll be so glad he didn't accidentally spend too much he'll agree to anything you say."

She laughed. "You're kind of devious. I'm almost ashamed to say how much I like that idea."

He lifted his chin. "You're welcome, *mamacita*. Always happy to help."

Still chuckling, Olivia began putting her plan together. Nick would be getting an email from her first thing in the morning.

Chapter Ten

*W*ith Katie at the wheel of her new pontoon, she and Sophie arrived at the dock at Bluewater Marina a few minutes before eleven. Uncle Hutch was due in at a quarter after. They'd offered to pick him up at the airport, but he'd told them he'd already booked an Uber.

Uncle Hutch was just that kind of guy. Always had been. Very self-sufficient, fearless, fun-loving, and willing to try anything at least once. Because of his music, he'd traveled the world, playing piano for more musicians than Katie had ever heard of. He'd even put out a few solo albums.

He was a wealth of stories, always ready with an easy smile and a kind word, and she knew without a shadow of a doubt that she would cry when she saw him.

Sophie helped tie up the boat. "It's been far too long."

"I know," Katie said as she cut the engine. "I feel bad about that, too. It's on us. We could have visited him anytime. We can't let so many years go by again."

"I agree." Sophie hopped out. "Why don't you get Owen to buy a place in New Orleans? Then we can go see him anytime we like."

Katie cut her eyes at her sister. "I have money, you know. So do you. We aren't without means."

"I know, but Owen wouldn't even notice. Hey, maybe he already has a place there. You think?"

Katie shrugged. She was learning that anything was possible when it came to billionaires. "Wouldn't surprise me. I'll ask him."

She climbed out beside her sister, and they headed up the dock toward the marina's office. It was closed, but the outside was lit up and there was a bench between the front door and the ice machine. They were just about to sit when a silver mid-size SUV pulled up alongside.

The back passenger door opened and a trim older man in tan trousers, a tropical blue shirt, linen jacket, and a straw hat climbed out. He was wearing blue suede shoes and a brilliant smile. "Katie-kins and Sophie-doll!"

"Uncle Hutch!" They spoke in unison, rushing forward to hug him.

He embraced them both. "My girls."

Katie welled up immediately. The smell of his bay rum aftershave brought back so many happy memories. She wiped at her eyes as she let go of him. "It's so good to see you."

"You, too. Both of you." He sighed with happiness. "You've gotten more beautiful. How is that possible?"

"Island life," Sophie said.

Katie was pleased to see her sister's eyes weren't exactly dry, either.

The Uber driver had gotten Uncle Hutch's things out of the back of the SUV and placed them nearby.

Uncle Hutch gave the man a nod. "Thanks, Tony. You have a good night, now."

"You, too, Mr. Hutch." The driver waved and climbed back into his vehicle.

Uncle Hutch had two suitcases and a carryon. As he picked up the smaller bag, Katie and Sophie each took one of the suitcases.

"We're going by boat," Sophie said. "Katie's boat. Owen bought it for her for Christmas."

"I heard," Uncle Hutch said. "That's quite a fella you've got there."

Katie grinned as they headed down the dock. "Wait until you meet him. You're going to love him."

"I can't wait. Although we've actually met before.

I played at a fundraiser he was at once. Years ago in Kansas City. He came over and shook the hand of everyone in the band. Can't recall what the fundraiser was for, though."

Katie shook her head. "You sure get around."

"That I do, my dear."

They got him and his bags onto the pontoon, made sure he was comfortably seated, then Katie started up the engine and headed for home. She was glad she'd spent the money to build Arthur's Marina. The dock was so much closer to where they lived than the one on the other side of the island.

She glanced back at Sophie and Uncle Hutch chatting away. He looked good. Whatever he was doing was working for him. Maybe being so active kept him young. He didn't look his age, at least not to her. More like a man in his sixties than one approaching eighty.

At the marina, Sophie helped her get the boat tied up again, then they each took one of his bags and headed for the house.

"Welcome to Compass Key," Katie said. "You'll get the ten-dollar tour tomorrow."

He shook his head as he took it all in. "I can't believe you girls live here now. What an adventure life must be living in a place like this."

Sophie laughed. "If you want to hear about an adventure, you should let Katie tell you how she met Owen."

He nodded. "I'd like to hear that very much. Maybe over a cup of tea?"

"We can arrange that," Katie said. "Might have some cake to go with it, if that interests you."

"Now, you know I have a sweet tooth," he said. "But I have to be able to fit into my suit for the wedding, too."

She snorted. "Uncle Hutch, you're in great shape."

"Well, then, just the one piece, I suppose."

They headed up the steps to the second level. Katie only worried about him for a couple of moments. He kept up with them just fine, and wasn't even out of breath when they reached the door.

"You're in *really* great shape." She knew she looked surprised, but she couldn't help it.

"I walk everywhere in New Orleans. Most everywhere I can, anyways. And playing with the Sly Cats is a pretty active job."

She unlocked the door and pushed it open, rolling his bag in ahead of her. She got the lights on as he and Sophie followed. "This is our place."

She'd already explained to him about their living

situation, about how Iris owned the house but they lived on the second floor and Nick and Jenny lived on the third.

He put his bag down and took a look around. "It's like a tropical treehouse. I love it. You must have some incredible views from up here."

"We sure do," Katie said.

"You'll see in the morning," Sophie added. "We'll have breakfast out there on the porch."

"Marvelous." He turned to face them again, gesturing toward the couch. "Is that for me, then?"

"No way," Sophie said. "You're in my room and I'm bunking with Katie."

"I don't want to take your bed."

"Too bad," Sophie said. "Because I'm not hearing any arguments. Decision's already been made."

He smiled. "You girls are too good to me."

"Come on," Sophie said. "I'll show you the room while Katie makes tea and gets the cake ready."

Katie nodded. "On it."

She was happier than she'd thought possible. Having Uncle Hutch here was such a gift. He was like the non-holiday version of Santa Claus. He had the kind of charm and charisma that gave him his own brand of magic. He was something special.

She was excited for Owen to meet him, excited to

introduce him to Josh and his family, and just blessed beyond measure to have so much family around her for the wedding.

She put her hand to her heart, overwhelmed by joy and feeling weepy again. Apparently, she was that kind of bride, the one who cried at every little thing.

That made her laugh. She wrote about those sorts of women! She went into the kitchen to put the kettle on and get the cake out of the fridge.

Sophie and Uncle Hutch joined her as she was putting slices of pineapple cake onto plates. Uncle Hutch had Fabio in his arms, and the cat was looking up at him adoringly.

Katie chuckled. "I see you found the only other man in the house."

"He's even handsomer than I remember. Aren't you, fella?" Uncle Hutch scratched Fabio under his chin, which caused Fabio to close his eyes and knead his paws in the air.

"He is." Katie opened the box that held the tea bags. "What kind of tea would you like?"

"Anything without caffeine is fine with me. I'm used to late nights but I'd like to get a little sleep." He put Fabio down and went over to the sliders to look out onto the side porch.

"I have a decaf orange pekoe."

"Perfect."

Sophie opened the sliders. "We can have our tea and cake outside if you like."

"That would be grand."

"Go have a seat," she said. "I'll bring it out to you."

As he went out, she joined Katie in the kitchen, her voice low. "I wish we could keep him here."

"Wouldn't that be something?" Katie stared toward the porch. "But he's not about to give up his life in New Orleans. And honestly, I think he'd be bored here."

"Yeah, I suppose."

But Katie wondered. What would it take for Uncle Hutch to make Compass Key his home?

Chapter Eleven

*L*eigh Ann padded down the steps to the kitchen, where Grant was already making coffee and whipping eggs. Thick slices of bacon sizzled in a pan on the stove. The smells alone were enough to make her fall in love with him all over again.

He smiled up at her. "Morning, beautiful."

"Hi, handsome." There were definite perks to cohabitating with a renaissance man like Grant. Breakfast was one of them. Although she hadn't been expecting it at this early hour. It was still dark outside, but her day began when her clients needed her. That was the trainer's life.

She tied her robe a little tighter before sitting at the counter. He put a cup of coffee in front of her, fixed just the way she liked it. She happily accepted it. "You're up early."

He shrugged. "I figured I'd get to the studio early. Catch that morning light."

She sipped her coffee. She had forty-five minutes before she had to be at the fitness center. "Thanks for this. I should probably take this back upstairs and drink it while I get my shower."

"I'll keep your plate warm."

"Thanks." She took her coffee back upstairs and got in the shower. She had Paul first thing for a session this morning, then she had a group yoga class, then a new guest, Julia Heston, for a private yoga lesson.

After that, she had a long break until Paul's weight training session. The next couple of weeks with him were going to be intense, but she knew that if she could get him results, he wouldn't be shy about sharing her name. Bringing in more celebrity guests would only raise the profile of the resort.

Always a good thing, in her book. It might also mean that she could increase the price of private sessions a little. Right now, they were lower than what most personal trainers charged because Leigh Ann hadn't been sure how popular they'd be. But that was no longer a worry.

She finished her shower, keeping it quick so she could get back downstairs, wrapped her hair in a towel to blow-dry after breakfast, then put on her usual uniform of capri leggings, sports bra, and Mother's Resort tank top. She'd ordered them from the same company where Olivia had gotten the rain jackets she'd given them all for Christmas.

One of the new things Leigh Ann had recently set up was a small retail space behind the front desk in the fitness center. Nothing major. T-shirts, tank tops, gym shorts, socks, and water bottles. All of it branded with the Mother's Resort logo. It was doing all right. And there was no better advertisement than actually wearing the gear that was on offer.

She laid her light jacket on the bed to grab later, then picked up her now empty mug and hustled back downstairs.

Grant was sitting at the counter, reading the local news on his tablet.

"Anything interesting?" she asked.

"There's a referendum coming up about adding an addition to the library in town."

She went to the coffee maker to refill her cup. "That's something I'd support."

"Me, too. In fact, I was thinking about donating a couple of signed prints to the fundraiser. I'm sure they'd give me a couple tickets to attend in exchange. You want to go with me?"

"I'd love to." She fixed her coffee. "I could talk to Grace, see if they could swing a dinner for two at either The Palms or Iris's."

"That would be fantastic. Even a signed cook-book from David and Chantelle would be great."

"I hadn't thought of that. Good idea. I'll ask Grace this afternoon. I have a little free time in between clients. I was thinking I'd come see you."

He grinned as he got up. "That's an equally fantastic plan. I'm about ready to have you sit for me again."

"Let me know when and I'll pencil you in."

"You're so busy these days. Which I know is a good thing, but I can't help but be a little jealous of the guests who get you to themselves for an entire hour." He took two plates out of the oven and put them on the counter. "Breakfast is served."

She brought her coffee to her seat, amused by his comment. "It's actually only fifty minutes, but you're welcome to schedule a session anytime you like."

"Thanks for reminding me that I need to up my workout game. Maybe I'll swing by the fitness center later." He sat next to her.

She leaned over and kissed his cheek. "You're in fantastic shape, as I can personally attest, and thank you for breakfast. If you want to work out, I'd be happy to help. If you need it."

"Sounds good. Anything for my muse." He winked at her as they dug in.

She made it to the fitness center with about three minutes to spare. She'd lingered longer than she should have at breakfast, but Grant was a hard guy to leave. Paul was already at the front desk, signing in. He had a water bottle in one hand and a towel over his shoulder. He was dressed in jogging pants and a T-shirt that featured the logo of *Ranger Dan, Danger Man*, one of the comedies he'd been in.

"Morning, Paul."

"Morning, Leigh Ann."

She tilted her head. "Did you lose more weight?"

He laughed. "I don't know. I'm not due to weigh in until tomorrow. But I hope so."

"I swear I can see it in your face."

"Fingers crossed you're right."

"Well, let's get to it." She headed for the private exercise room. "How are you feeling this morning? Still sore?"

"I am, but I know this session will help that a lot."

"Are you hydrated?"

"I've had black coffee, which I know isn't ideal, but I've also had some water with electrolytes." He held up his water bottle. "I have more with me, too. Never had any idea how important electrolytes were until Kendall told me about them."

Leigh Ann nodded as she opened the door and switched on the lights. "Amazing what a difference they make, right?" She turned on the soft background music she used for yoga, then went to the rack to grab a mat for him.

She laid it out, lit the candles on either side of the table where she kept the small gong she used to end most sessions, then dimmed the lights a touch to set a relaxing mood. "All right, let's begin."

She led him through two rounds of sun salutations, slightly modified with some longer holds, before moving onto floor work and the positions that would help open his hips, stretch out his back and legs, and finally into some others meant to relax the body and allow for healing.

In the last few minutes, she led him through savasana, a calming position also known as corpse pose, although she didn't often share that term with her older guests. The pose of being prone on the floor allowed the mind and body to relax as one. From that state, meditation could easily be entered, although a lot of people fell asleep.

Paul let out a soft snore.

She pressed her lips together to keep from laughing. She kneeled down beside him to gently shake his shoulder. The fact that she was trying to wake up

Paul De Luca, Hollywood superstar, made the moment slightly surreal.

"Paul? We're all done. Paul?"

His eyes flickered open. "Oh, sorry. Did I drift off?"

She nodded. "You did but that's all right. A lot of people do during savasana."

He sat up. "I fall asleep during a lot of massages, too."

"So do I. It's pretty common. I think it's a good sign that you're able to relax that deeply."

He got to his feet, taking a long drink from his water bottle. "I like that you always find the silver lining. You're such a positive person, Leigh Ann. You're so easy to be around, you know? I get that some trainers think they have to be all hardcore and they can't be too friendly, because that's showing weakness or some other crap, but not you."

"Well, thanks. I think it's very possible to be both kind and firm. But then, I come from a yoga background. Most of us in that discipline tend to favor a certain amount of gentleness in everything we do. Doesn't mean we're pushovers, but—"

"No, not at all. And I didn't mean to imply that in the slightest." He looked a little worried, like he'd offended her.

"I didn't get that from you. I took what you said as a great compliment."

He smiled. "Okay. Good. Because that's how I meant it. I really do like you, Leigh Ann."

"You're a great client, Paul." She hoped using the word "client" made it clear that she hoped he only meant he liked her as a trainer.

But before there was a chance for any more discussion, he leaned in and kissed her.

Chapter Twelve

Iris postponed her morning walk around the island so that she could see Nick before he went into his office, which was located in the same building as the spa. It was the same medical office shared by Peter, one of the massage therapists who was also a paramedic and had been their main medical person on staff until Nick's arrival.

Nick had said he'd stop in on his way and, true to his word, it was eight-thirty when he knocked on the door.

Vera let him in. Iris was getting a cup of coffee in the kitchen when he entered. He looked so reassuring in his tan pants and pastel plaid shirt, his doctor's bag in one hand. "Good morning, Dr. Nick."

"Morning, Iris. Vera. How are you ladies doing today?" He shut the door behind him.

"Just fine," Iris said. "Can I get you a cup of coffee?"

"Sure, I'd love one."

"Take a seat," Vera said to Iris. "I'll bring it over."

Iris took her cup into the living room, thankful that Vera was in on the real reason Nick was here. She sat in her chair, gesturing for Nick to take a spot on the couch. He did. She smiled at him. "Thank you for coming by this morning. I know you're a busy man."

"You're welcome. You'll always be a priority for me, Iris. I want you to know that, for you, I am never too busy." He grinned. "Even if you are one of the healthiest people living on this island now."

She laughed. "In no small part thanks to you."

"Just living up to the oath I took. Are you still feeling good?"

"I'm feeling great."

"Glad to hear that."

Vera came over with his coffee and set it down on the table, then took a seat in the other chair. Iris almost laughed. She'd figured Vera would find a way to be busy in the kitchen during this chat, but she admired the woman's bold decision to just join them.

He took a sip of his coffee. "Thanks, Vera, this hits the spot." He looked at Iris again. "What can I do for you?"

Iris narrowed her eyes and lifted her chin, her standard expression for dealing with a guest on the verge of bad behavior. Or young men she needed to tell her the truth. "You can explain to me just exactly what is going on with your mother's early arrival."

Nick hesitated, a deer in the headlights for a split second, then he shifted his gaze to his cup. "We're dealing with her."

"Nick," Iris said softly. "If she's causing you problems..."

He looked up and shook his head. "It's nothing we can't deal with. I know she's not the easiest person to be around, but she just wants to feel included."

"And your bride-to-be feels the same way about this? That your mother wanting to be included is something she can deal with?"

He blinked like that was a question he hadn't even considered. "Sure. Yes. Jenny's not one to just go along. She speaks up for herself."

Maybe so, Iris thought. But shouldn't Nick be doing some of that, too? Yolanda was his mother. Iris sighed. "I don't mean to overstep but I only want the best for you and Jenny. I've come to think of you both as family. To me, that's exactly what you are. You're Arthur's son and if you don't think that gives you a special place in my heart, then please understand that it does."

Nick smiled. "Thank you. I feel the same way

about you. And I know you want the best for us. You wouldn't have let us move into your home if you felt differently. I value your input. And your concern. But I promise, everything is fine. Maybe a little less fine than it would have been if my mother had shown up closer to the wedding, but you can't fault her for wanting to be involved."

Iris shook her head. "No, I can't. What mother wouldn't want to be? I take it you've included Olivia, too, then? What's fair is fair, right?"

He opened his mouth, shut it again, then finally spoke. "We haven't really. I mean, Jenny has, some-what. But we've been trying to do as much of the planning ourselves as we can. It's not like it's a big wedding. Jenny seems to have everything under control. Every time I ask her how it's going, she says fine."

Iris snorted. "My dear boy. You really have no idea how much goes into a wedding, do you? Have you even had one conversation with Amanda about this? Planning weddings is a big part of what she does. If you haven't, you should, because I think you're fooling yourself if you believe Jenny doesn't need more help."

"I haven't spoken to Amanda. But you make a good point. I'll go see her today, I promise." He shrugged, looking slightly lost. "I just figured if Jenny needed help, she'd say something."

"Back to your mother for a moment." Iris took a drink of coffee. "I know your relationship with her is better than it was. But I worry that she's using that goodwill to make waves. Waves Jenny might be struggling to keep her head above. Please, don't let your mother come between you two."

Nick frowned, making Iris think she'd pushed too much. "I'd never do that, Iris. I wouldn't. I love Jenny. She's the one. There's no question about that. No one is going to come between us."

"Good." She held her hands up. "I've said my piece. All out of love for you both, I assure you."

He seemed to relax a little. "I know. Thank you. I should run. As it so happens, Olivia asked to see me this morning, too, so I need to get to her office."

Iris wondered what that was about. "Better go, then. Don't want to keep your future mother-in-law waiting."

"No." He smiled, but it was tight and didn't reach his eyes. "Thank you for the coffee. Have a good day."

"You, too." She stayed in her chair as he left, her gaze shifting to Vera. "You've been awfully quiet."

Vera was looking at the couch where Nick had

been. "I don't think he was completely pleased to hear all of that. But I think you've given him a lot to mull over. A few things he hadn't considered."

"I overstepped a little, maybe" Iris picked up her mug, holding it in both hands. "But if anything were to happen to those two and I hadn't said anything, I'd be mad as a hornet, so I'm not sorry."

Vera sat forward, nodding. "I hope he opens his eyes a little more and sees what's really going on, because if Yolanda *isn't* up to something, I'll bake her a cake."

Chapter Thirteen

Olivia was nervous about talking to Nick. She didn't love confrontation, but she wasn't going to let a little discomfort stand in the way of her daughter's mental well-being. Nick needed to know what was going on.

And Jenny needed to be protected from the overbearing woman who was his mother. Why on Earth had Yolanda decided to arrive so early? Why couldn't she have just stayed with the original plan? Olivia found that kind of behavior extremely frustrating.

At nine a.m. on the dot, there was a knock on her door. Olivia saved her work on the computer and took her reading glasses off. "Come in."

It opened and Nick walked through. "Morning."

He wasn't quite smiling. In fact, he looked nervous. "Morning, Nick." She folded her glasses and used them to point to the chairs across from her desk before putting the glasses on the desk in front of her. "Have a seat."

"Thanks." He sat, but not all the way back. Like

he might need to get up quickly. "Is everything all right? I hope I'm not here because the medical department is having financial troubles."

Olivia leaned back in her chair. "No, the medical department's accounting is balancing just fine. Nothing to worry about there. This isn't work-related, I can assure you."

He smiled, then didn't. "Then it's personal?"

"Yes. It's about Jenny." She paused for a long second. "And your mother."

"Oh, boy." He shoved a hand through his hair.

"I take it you already know that your mother is interfering with the wedding planning, then?"

He looked up suddenly. "Interfering? No, I didn't know that. Although Iris asked me to come see her this morning, too. I just left her place. And basically it was about my mother and about Jenny being stressed out by all the work she's doing."

"Iris is a very perceptive woman." Who could probably hear some of what was going on, thanks to living in the same dwelling and spending a lot of time on her porch. "That's exactly what this conversation is going to be about. Jenny came to see me last night, in tears because of all of this and because she asked me *not* to talk to your mother, I'm talking to you."

Nick's brows bent and concern filled his eyes. "Jenny was crying?"

"She's very stressed. And your mother isn't helping. You have to know that."

"I knew my mom had made a couple suggestions, but I explained to her that we're on a budget and things are what they are because of that."

Olivia nodded slowly. "That's good, but it doesn't seem to have stopped your mother from butting in. I know that's not the kindest language, but it's what she's doing. With the PR work Jenny's doing in addition to planning the wedding, she's close to breaking. I'm not going to allow my daughter to struggle like this, do you understand?"

"Of course." He nodded, swallowing. "I don't want her to go through that, either. What can I do?"

"First of all, you're going to talk to your mother and you're going to tell her very clearly that if she makes another wedding-related suggestion to Jenny, there will be repercussions. My suggestion is that she leaves the island until it's actually time for the wedding."

Nick frowned. "That's a little harsh, don't you think?"

Elbows on the arms of the chair, Olivia steepled

her fingers before her. Her nerves about talking to him were gone, replaced by the fierce need to protect her daughter. "Your mother's last suggestion to Jenny was that Jenny wear her wedding dress to get married in."

His eyes rounded. Olivia kept going. "Do you know how long Jenny and I looked for her dress? Do you have any idea how much she loves the dress she finally found? Your mother told her that her dress looked cheap and that her own dress was a much better option." Something Jenny had only revealed later, after Olivia had pressed her a little more.

His mouth came open. "That's...I didn't know that."

"Don't you think it's odd that your mother brought her wedding dress with her? Who does that?"

His face scrunched up a little. "It is sort of strange. Or...very strange."

"To me, that makes her interference premeditated. Yolanda arrived early so she could cause trouble."

"I don't know if that's..." He groaned. "No, you're right. That's probably why she came early." He looked frustrated, which Olivia thought was a fairly understandable response. "Why didn't Jenny tell me about all of this?"

"Because Yolanda is your mother. And about to be her mother-in-law. Jenny didn't want to cause any issues between you two right before the wedding. She's knows that you're still working on your relationship with your mom." Olivia put her hands down and leaned forward. "But unlike my daughter, I don't have the same concerns. If your relationship with your mother fails, that's on her. If your relationship with my daughter fails because of your mother, that's on both of you. Do I make myself clear?"

"Yes, perfectly." He nodded quickly. "I swear, I had no idea. And no idea Jenny was so stressed. She hides it really well."

"She had years of practice living with an alcoholic father. Even if she didn't understand that he was drinking, she knew there was strife between her dad and me."

Nick huffed out a breath. "I feel like a terrible fiancé. I had some idea that my mother was trying to help, but no clue it was like this. And that it wasn't really help." He glanced at his watch. "I have a patient coming in at ten but after that, I'm going to deal with this."

"I'm glad to hear that."

His jaw set and he shook his head. "She won't like it, but I'm going to find her a hotel on the mainland and move her over there today. No matter what she says."

Olivia's brows shot up. She hadn't expected that. "Really?"

He nodded. "Jenny's happiness and well-being are everything to me. If I can't protect her from stuff like this now, what does that say about me as a man? And a husband?" He looked away. "I owe you an apology, too. You shouldn't have had to come to me with this. I should have known. I should have paid more attention. Like I do with my patients."

"I know you're busy—"

"That's not a great excuse. Everyone's busy. I'm sorry. I'm going to make this right."

Olivia smiled. He was stepping up. She loved him even more for that. "Thank you, Nick."

He got to his feet. "Iris suggested I talk to Amanda, too. About what it takes to plan a wedding, because clearly I have no idea. Do you think it's too late to get her to help us?"

Olivia shook her head. "I think Amanda would do whatever she could to lighten Jenny's load. Just talk to her."

"I'll pay her whatever she wants."

"Didn't she offer to plan the wedding for you as an engagement gift?"

His brow furrowed. "I suppose she did. Which makes us both dumb for not taking her up on it."

"Go talk to her. See what she can do. Better late then never, right?"

"I hope so." He stuck his hand out. "Thank you."

She got up and came around the desk, arms wide. "I think we can do better than a handshake."

He smiled and hugged her. "Does this mean you're not mad at me?"

She hugged him tighter. "I was never mad at you. Just concerned about Jenny."

His smile was gone as she pulled away. He nodded. "That makes two of us."

Chapter Fourteen

Katie was still in her robe when she went out to the kitchen to start the coffee. Uncle Hutch was already there, the smell of coffee in the air, and he had a cup in his hand. He was standing by the sliders looking out at the water.

She cleared her throat softly. "Morning."

"Morning, Katie-kins. I hope I didn't wake you."

"Nope. I had no idea you were up. Thanks for making coffee."

"You're welcome." He was dressed in a pair of track pants, a T-shirt, and a matching track jacket. With sneakers. "I was thinking I might go out for a walk. See the place."

"If you give me time to change, I'll go with you. Sophie's still sleeping."

"That would be grand. I'll be right here."

Katie made a half cup of coffee and took it back to the bedroom. Quietly, so as not to wake Sophie, she changed into leggings, a T-shirt, and sneakers. She pulled her hair into a ponytail, then popped on a ballcap. All the while taking sips of her very hot coffee.

But it was enough to get her going. And the chance to walk with Uncle Hutch and show him the island was all the motivation she needed, really.

She grabbed her phone and stuck it in the pocket of her leggings, then took her cup with her, closing the bedroom door as she went out.

She drained the last bit of coffee, put the cup by the sink so she could reuse it when they got back, and walked toward the door. "Ready to go."

"So am I." Uncle Hutch joined her and together they went out and down the steps at the side of the house.

As they reached the bottom of the steps, Iris was coming out her front door. She gave them a smile. "Morning."

"Iris!" Katie put her hand on her uncle's arm. "This is my uncle, Emerson Hutch. Uncle Hutch, this is Iris Cotton, who I've told you all about."

Uncle Hutch bent at the waist in a courtly bow. "It's my pleasure to meet you, Mrs. Cotton. I've heard so many wonderful things about you."

Iris laughed. "Well, I hope I can live up to them."

"The only thing my niece didn't tell me was what

a beauty you are." He smiled, sticking out his chest a little.

Katie barely stifled a giggle.

"Oh my," Iris said, putting her hand to her heart. "You're quite the charmer, aren't you."

"Just a teller of the truth, fair lady. But I suppose we're holding you up. My apologies."

Iris shook her head, her cheeks a little pink. "I was just about to go for my morning walk."

"We're about to do the same thing," Uncle Hutch said. "Maybe we could join you? If that wouldn't be too much of an imposition."

Iris's eyes were sparkling in a way Katie wasn't sure she'd seen before. "I'd love the company." She looked at Katie. "You don't mind, do you?"

"Not at all." Katie was amused by the whole thing. Uncle Hutch was a known charmer and it was fun to see Iris light up the way she had. "Who better to give a tour of Compass Key than the woman who built it."

"Well, then," Iris said. "Let's be on our way."

"Marvelous." Uncle Hutch offered his arm as they came together on the path and Iris took it.

She immediately launched into the tour. "I didn't build this place alone, you understand. My late husband, Arthur, and I did it together."

"I've only seen a small portion of it," Uncle Hutch said. "But I can already see he was a man of vision."

"Oh, he was," Iris agreed.

As the pair chatted, Katie fell into step behind them, smiling because she couldn't help it. The two of them together were very sweet. Iris was happy to point out all sorts of things about the resort, sharing little stories about when a building was built or how a certain design feature came to be.

Uncle Hutch complimented all of it with genuine sincerity, seemingly impressed by everything Iris showed him. They passed the first stretch of bungalows, then detoured by the adults-only pool to walk past the main building before heading toward the guest marina.

Iris held onto his arm the whole time.

They went by the marina, stopping briefly to walk out onto the dock so Uncle Hutch could have a better look at the water, which he proclaimed to be as blue as the color blue should be. From there, they went on through to the newest section of the resort, Phase II.

The landscaping sparkled with color and sweet scents carried past them on the breeze. Further in, they came to the family bungalows, then the aquatic area.

The pool and lazy river weren't super busy yet, but everyone using them looked happy. The kids especially. Castaways was open, offering simple breakfast fare, and the aroma of coffee greeted them.

Uncle Hutch smiled at it all. "What a beautiful place this is."

"Thank you," Iris said. "But I can't take the credit. This was all the girls' doing. They orchestrated this whole section. I agree, they did a tremendous job."

"You certainly knew what you were doing when you brought them on."

"Now that," Iris said with pride in her eyes, "I will take credit for."

Uncle Hutch stopped after a few more steps and pointed up. "You've got your name on a building. What's that all about?"

Iris leaned into him ever so slightly. "That was a Christmas gift from the girls. They named the new restaurant after me. Wasn't that sweet?" She grinned at Katie, who came alongside her. "The most wonderful surprise."

Katie smiled back. "That was a fun day when we revealed that to you."

"Say," Iris said. "We should have dinner there tonight. What do you think?"

"Fine with me," Uncle Hutch said.

"Oh, um." Katie hated to be the bearer of bad news. "I've got Josh and Christy coming in today with the kids. There's going to be a lot more of us."

"So?" Iris shrugged. "Doesn't Iris's have a private room?"

Katie nodded. "It does but it might be booked." It seemed like a big imposition to her. Not to mention the cost. Which she could afford, she reminded herself. But she didn't want anyone else to feel obligated. Anyone like Owen. She knew he would. He always wanted to pay. But this was almost entirely her family.

"Well, let's go in and ask."

"I don't think they're open yet." Katie pulled out her phone. "Let me text Grace."

She typed out a note with the request then hit Send.

"Thank you," Iris said. "I know I'm imposing myself on your family but—"

"Iris, you are part of my family." Katie meant it, too. "Don't think otherwise."

Her phone, still in her hand, vibrated. She paraphrased the text that had just come in from Grace. "Grace says the room is available and do we want it." She nodded at her phone. "I guess we do." She looked up. "Six o'clock all right? I know Josh and Christy like to get the kids in bed no later than eight."

"That's fine with me," Uncle Hutch said.

"Me, too," Iris added.

Katie started typing an answer to Grace, then paused. "How many are we going to be? I need to figure that out." Herself and Owen, Sophie, Gage, Josh, Christy, the two kids, Uncle Hutch, and Iris. That was...ten. She added that information to the text and hit Send.

Owen's parents and sister weren't coming in until the day of the wedding.

Done, came Grace's quick response. *The room holds fifteen, so you're good to go. And of of course, the owner discount applies.*

Thanks! Katie hadn't factored that in but that would give her an excuse for Owen not to pay. If he did, she'd tell him the discount wouldn't apply. Would he buy that? Probably not. But whatever. She looked at Iris and her uncle. "Dinner is all set. Guess I'd better make sure the rest of the group knows about it."

"This is going to be so much fun," Iris said. "Although now we probably ought to get home and have some breakfast. Have you eaten, Emerson?"

"Not yet."

Katie chimed in. "Sophie is making a breakfast casserole this morning. Would you like to join us, Iris? I'm sure there will be plenty." She got the sense that Iris was eager to spend a bit more time with Uncle Hutch. Katie was happy to help work that out. Who was she to stand in the way of a new friendship? Or possibly more.

"That would be lovely. I'll see if Vera can't whip up a little fruit salad or something for me to bring."

"Well, then, let's get a move on," Katie said. "Lead us home, Iris."

Iris smiled and patted Uncle Hutch's arm. "We'll go through the staff housing area. Right this way."

Katie kept up her pace behind them while texting Sophie to fill her in. Once Katie had sent all of that, she put her phone back in her pocket and returned to watching the pair in front of her.

Was there any chance that this might be a budding romance? Uncle Hutch had never been married. He'd had a few girlfriends, but none that were really serious. He'd always said the life of a musician was just too hard on relationships.

With the way he was smiling, Katie had to wonder if he still thought that was true.

Chapter Fifteen

*G*race entered Katie's special reservation into the restaurant's computer system as soon as she got in. She was happy Katie and her family were all coming. The private room had been added with the thinking that it would be good to have for smaller wedding parties or large families, which was all it had been used for so far.

It was designed with a wall of frosted glass doors so that it could be hidden away when not in use, but easily opened and added to the restaurant's general seating when needed. They usually did that on the weekends, when outside guests were allowed in.

With the reservation on the books, she left the hostess stand to go to the small office in the back of the kitchen. There, she settled in to go over schedules, inventory, and ordering. Looking over things daily meant no backlog, and fewer chances of mistakes.

Katie and Owen's wedding was not being held on Compass Key, so there wasn't anything for the restaurant staff to prepare for. She had no idea where the wedding was going to be. Owen had taken control of that aspect of things, along with the meal, the cake, and the reception.

Grace was dying to know what he had planned. It wasn't going to be a big wedding. Maybe thirty people altogether. That could mean all sorts of things for the location.

Might he be flying them all somewhere? That would be interesting. It was so hard to tell with a man like that. She eagerly awaited the wedding day. Just two days from now.

Getting to attend with David would be a special treat. They didn't get to go to many things as a couple because of his late hours, but he'd arranged to have that whole day off. With the way everything was going and with the training he'd been doing with his cooks, she had no worries.

The restaurants had come a long way in the year since David and she had taken over things. Granted, there had only been The Palms and the snack and smoothie bar by the pool at first. There was a lot more now. But they'd more than doubled the staff and operations were running smoothly.

She knocked on the wooden desktop for good measure. No point in jinxing anything.

She wasn't quite halfway through her work when

the office door opened, and David came in. She grinned and pushed back from the desk, rolling her chair away so she had room to get up, which she did, and leaned over the desk to kiss him. "Hiya."

"Hey." He kissed her back. "How's your day going?"

"Good. Katie and all of her family will be in for dinner tonight in the private room."

He nodded. "Any special requests?"

"No, but I know they'll have two kids with them. Well, one's still a baby, but the older one will probably eat."

He shrugged. "No big deal. We have a kids menu now, so shouldn't be an issue."

"Any idea about the specials this evening?"

"A fresh catch of some kind, for sure, maybe scallops, but could be grouper. We'll definitely have a steak, too. I need to look through the walk-ins and see if anything speaks to me. I'll let you know once I've figured it out."

"Sounds good."

"We're doing a hot soup, too. Our cooler weather will be gone soon, but until then, I'm going to take advantage and do something interesting. Italian wedding soup for both here and at The Palms. How's that sound?"

"Like something I want a bowl of for lunch."

He laughed. "I'm not sure it'll be ready by then, but I'll see what I can do."

"Thanks."

He left and she went back to work. Just getting through the schedules was a big task. Curt wrote them up for Castaways and Iris's, but then she had to check them and approve them, mostly to make sure that no one was getting too much overtime. A little was okay, when the need arose, but too much and Grace would have Olivia to answer to about why they'd gone over budget.

She also checked to make sure there were no conflicts. Curt was pretty good with scheduling, but every once in a while, she'd find someone had been double-booked. Or in one case, booked to work the same shift at both Iris's and The Palms. Each restaurant had its own staff, but there were a few people who overlapped to get more hours and help fill in when another employee needed time off.

By the time she'd finished with those, then started on the inventory sheets, it was almost one in the afternoon. Her stomach was rumbling. Breakfast had been a quick bowl of oatmeal this morning and it hadn't done much for her. She needed protein, but she could already smell the woodsmoke coming from Castaways. It was making her mouth water.

If she ate pizza for lunch every day, she was going to need the next size up in shorts. That would not do. But the pizza smelled so good. Maybe she'd just have a salad. Not the most exciting option, but probably the healthiest.

She was about to get up and see about that salad when the office door opened again. David came in carrying a big, squat mug on a large saucer that also held a toasted slice of crusty bread. "Italian wedding soup, just like you ordered."

"Seriously? That was fast."

He snorted. "It wasn't that fast. Plus, I already had stock made. Those little meatballs don't take much time at all. And the pasta..." He shrugged. "It's not too hard to whip it up pretty quick when you know what you're doing."

"Which you do."

"I like to think so." He put the soup on her desk but hovered nearby. "Taste it and tell me what you think."

She already knew it would be good but she did as he asked. It was better than good. It was delicious. "It's perfect. What did you do? There's something different about it. A little kick of acid, right? But also something else."

He smiled and nodded. "You always have had a superior palate. Yep. I added a little lemon juice, some dried lemon zest but also a touch of fennel pollen."

"It's the best version of this soup I've ever had."

"Well, since it's tonight's soup, along with the usual conch chowder, I hope the guests think so, too. The specials are done. Orange-glazed scallop and shrimp skewers over rice with roasted Brussels sprouts, and then surf-and-turf of a filet mignon paired with a Florida lobster tail. Catch of the day is golden pompano in both restaurants. Here at Iris's, we're doing it with a white wine beurre blanc, fried capers, and diced heirloom tomatoes. That'll have whipped potatoes and asparagus with it as well."

She moaned at how good those dishes sounded. "Somehow, I'm eating but getting hungrier. Those sound great."

He tipped his head in appreciation. "I'm glad you approve."

The phone rang.

He grabbed the door handle. "I'll let you get back to work."

"Thanks." She picked up the receiver. "Iris's, this

is Grace speaking."

"Miss Grace? It's Elizabeth. I'm sorry but I can't come in tonight. I have a fever and chills and I'm just sick as a dog. I'm –" Her words ended in a violent sneeze.

Grace jerked back at the sound, then quickly put the receiver back to her ear. "Don't worry about it. You just rest and get better. I'll take care of it."

"Thank you." Elizabeth sneezed again as she hung up.

Thankfully, germs didn't travel across phone lines. Grace pulled up the day's schedule to see who wasn't on that might be able to pick up Elizabeth's shift. With Katie's big group coming in, they couldn't be stretched too thin.

She ate while she made phone calls to see who could cover the shift, but everyone she talked to had plans or was already scheduled at The Palms. It was possible one of the lunch crew might be able to work a double, but she'd have to talk to them. And she hated to work anyone that hard.

By the time her soup mug was empty, the solution was clear.

Even if someone could work a double, Grace was going to have to stay and provide backup. Maybe she'd just take care of Katie's group herself.

Chapter Sixteen

*J*enny hadn't expected Nick home for lunch, but she was really glad to see him. At least with him in the house, his mom would chill out a bit. She needed the break, too, because right before he'd shown up, Yolanda had been pushing Jenny to try her wedding dress on again. It was so that, in Yolanda's words, Jenny could see how much classier it was.

Jenny had been doing her best to be kind about it, but it was a losing battle. How did Yolanda not understand that there was no way Jenny's body was going to fill that dress? Yolanda had to be a D cup. Or bigger. Whatever extra-large size money could buy.

Jenny, on the other hand, was a nice, natural C. But being unable to fill out her almost-mother-in-law's dress didn't even make the top ten of why Jenny didn't want to wear it. The dress was not in the least bit Jenny's style. It was awful. Low-cut, with puffy sleeves and all kinds of glittery appliques and sheer panels on the torso that made it look like something a Vegas showgirl would have worn to get married in.

Maybe that was what Yolanda had been going for?

Then Nick walked in, ending the discussion, and Jenny had given him a bigger hug than usual. Yolanda had said hello, and gone out to the porch. He'd excused himself to make a few phone calls and Jenny had gone right to work after that, making sandwiches from the chicken salad she'd prepared for that purpose. Rotisserie chickens from the local Publix were not only a good buy when on sale, but useful in so many ways.

She whipped up three sandwiches on seeded wheat bread, put a pickle spear on each plate, then added some carrot sticks to hers and a small handful of chips to Nick's and Yolanda's plates. She carried them to the table.

Yolanda stayed on the porch reading a gossip magazine the whole time Jenny was in the kitchen. Would have been nice if Yolanda had offered to help, but Jenny figured it was probably better she hadn't. It would have just been another opportunity for her to criticize Jenny or the food or *something*.

Jenny was in the kitchen filling three glasses with iced tea when Nick came back. "Phone calls all done?"

He nodded. "There's a conference that has asked me to speak."

She put the pitcher of iced tea down. "Really?"

"They're associated with the organization I went overseas with, Medical United. They'd like me to come talk about my experiences."

"That's pretty cool. When is it?"

"Next year. In Chicago. I don't want to go unless you go with me, though. It'll be a short trip. Probably just three days. But I thought it might be nice to get away by ourselves."

"I would love to go." She smiled. "Thanks."

He came a little closer. "Listen, I need you to tell me the truth about something."

He looked so serious, a tiny bit of worry crept into her. "Of course."

"Is my mother being a hindrance? Is she stressing you out?"

Jenny glanced toward the porch, then sighed. "I really didn't want to say anything. It's not a big deal, but she has been making a lot of comments. And... trying to get me to wear her wedding dress."

He stared past her to the porch. "But it *is* a big deal, isn't it? Tell me the truth. Please."

A pit opened up in Jenny's stomach. She really

didn't want to be the bad guy but she didn't want to lie to Nick, either. "It hasn't been great having her here. She's kind of making me miserable with all her little comments. She says things when you're not here that I don't think she'd say otherwise."

He took her face in his hands and kissed her, then leaned his forehead against hers. "I'm so sorry. That's inexcusable. I don't want you stressed out. In fact, I went to see Amanda before I came home and she assured me she'll do whatever you need her to do to make this wedding happen. Please tell me you'll call her and take her up on her offer?"

"I don't know what she could—"

"She can call vendors, confirm that they're all set up, coordinate any last-minute things, all sorts of stuff. Look, I know you're a very capable woman. But you don't have to prove it by singlehandedly planning this wedding on your own."

She exhaled and sank into his arms. "Okay. I'll talk to her. I've just felt compelled to do this myself. I don't really know why. Maybe to prove that I could? Maybe because I figured everyone else was already so busy that I didn't want to impose? Maybe because we're already getting the location for free? But if Amanda wants to help, then I'll let her."

"Thank you." He gave her another hug, then let go of her. "Now I need to tell my mother she's moving to the mainland for the remainder of her stay."

"What?" His words shocked her. She'd never imagined he'd do that.

He nodded. "I've already found a place for her and booked it."

Jenny could have fallen over she was so surprised. "She's going to pitch a fit."

"She'll get over it if she wants to attend the wedding at all."

"You're serious."

"I am." He looked at her. "I'm not going to have you in a bad place because of her. I know all too well what she's capable of and I'm sorry that her nonsense has already affected you. But that ends today."

"You don't want to try just talking to her? Maybe she'll behave if she sees how serious you are."

"No. She had every chance to act right when she first got here. Which I thought she would, given that we're supposed to be mending things between us. But clearly she came here with an agenda and I'm not having it."

Jenny didn't know what else to say. She felt bad

for Yolanda, but proud of Nick. And so in love with him it made her heart ache. Yolanda had done this to herself, though. He was right that if she'd just been nice, none of this would be happening. Jenny grabbed his arm. "How did you know all of this was going on?"

"I had two interesting conversations today with Iris and your mom." He shook his head. "I understand why you didn't tell me what she was doing, but you should have come to me, sweetheart. You're everything to me. You understand that?"

She smiled. If she hadn't before, she certainly did now. "Yes, I do. I'm sorry I didn't tell you. I just didn't want to ruin things between you."

"You didn't ruin them. She did." He sighed. "Now I need to go talk to her."

"Okay. Wait. Shouldn't we eat lunch first?"

He shook his head. "I'm not going to be able to sit there and pretend like nothing's wrong. I'm sorry. I know you went to the trouble of making that food."

"It's no big deal. I just don't think she'll want to eat after."

"I guess we'll see soon enough."

She watched him walk out to the porch. She could only imagine the fireworks that were about to go off. There was no way Yolanda would take this calmly.

But this was between her and Nick. Jenny wasn't getting involved. The kitchen was a fine vantage point. She quietly began to clean up what little mess there was as she listened, the words drifting in through the open sliding doors.

"Mom? Listen, I've decided it would be best for you to move to a hotel on the mainland until the wedding."

As best as Jenny could tell, Yolanda was staring up at him. "What? Why?"

"You know why. You've been saying unkind things to Jenny about the wedding. I can't have you here making her feel bad and stressing her out. It's not a healthy situation."

"That's not true." She put her hands on the arms of the chair, like she was about to get up. "I've done nothing of the kind."

He took a breath. "I already know what you've done. I'm not asking for confirmation. And frankly, I'm disappointed you'd lie about it. Not surprised, just disappointed. Now, you can come in and eat lunch with us and then after that you can get packed up and I'll take you over to the hotel where I've made you a reservation, or you're free to skip lunch and just pack up immediately. Either way, I'm having lunch with my fiancée."

He walked back inside, came to the kitchen and picked up two of the glasses of iced tea, took them to the table, and sat down.

Yolanda stomped through the sliders in her high-heeled sandals. She glared at Jenny. "You're a liar."

Jenny bobbed her head back in shock. "I've only told the truth."

Nick jumped up and immediately took a position between Jenny and his mother. "Get your things packed. We're leaving now."

Yolanda's face was turning red. "I can't believe you'd pick her and this place over me."

He just stared at her. "What happened to you? I thought we worked all of this out at Christmas. Why have you become so mean and selfish again?"

Yolanda's lower lip quivered. "Because you've left me!"

"I haven't left you. I've grown up and moved on. It's called being an adult and living a life." He stood his ground. "Go pack. Or I'll do it for you."

She took one look at Jenny, then stormed past Nick to her room, slamming the door when she went in.

With a long sigh, he turned to face Jenny. "I'm so sorry."

She went to him and hugged him. "You have nothing to apologize for. I'm sorry things worked out this way, though."

She felt him nod. "Me, too."

Chapter Seventeen

*A*manda wasn't surprised to hear from Jenny, not after talking with Nick earlier. "Like I told Nick, I'm happy to help in whatever way you need me. I know from firsthand experience how stressful and draining it can be to plan a wedding. Especially when you're the bride!"

Jenny let out a little sigh. "I feel like a fool for not calling you earlier. For not taking you up on your offer to help. I guess I'm just a little stubborn sometimes."

"Who isn't?" Amanda smiled into the phone. "I think it would be best if we could meet in person so you can show me what you've got. That will save you from having to text or email me massive amounts of information, too."

"That would be great." Her exhale sounded like the release of a thousand pounds of stress. "I am so relieved. I cannot thank you enough. Can we meet over there? I could come now. I know this isn't work-related, so I don't expect you to give me your undivided attention."

"Please come. If I have to take a phone call or two, I will, but Carissa is here, so it's not like I'm manning the front desk all alone."

"I will be there in ten minutes."

"Perfect."

Jenny was true to her word, arriving shortly with a tote bag full of odds and ends. She slumped into one of the guest chairs in the office as though just being there was already helping her relax. "Thank you again. And thank you for not making me feel worse than I already do."

"I would never do that."

Jenny nodded. "I know you wouldn't. You're too nice for that. All of my mom's friends are. Too bad..."

Jenny started to cry softly.

Amanda's eyes widened. She hadn't been expecting that. She got up, moved to the chair next to Jenny, then sat and embraced the young woman. "Let it all out. Sometimes a good cry is just what you need to destress."

Jenny shook her head. "It's not that. It's just that..."

Amanda handed her the box of tissues from the desk.

Jenny took one and blew her nose. "It's Yolanda.

Nick's mom. Everything kind of exploded this afternoon and that was not my intention."

"Of course it wasn't. What happened?"

Jenny explained everything that had gone on, all the comments Yolanda had made, right down to Nick basically escorting his mother out of the house and taking her to a hotel on the mainland.

"Wow." Amanda just blinked. She'd thought *her* mother was bad. Sometimes it was good to get perspective. "I understand more than you know."

"I know you do. I know you've had issues with your own mother."

"I have. We're slowly working through them, but every day I wonder if today will be the day she decides it's too much effort. Sounds like that might be what happened with Yolanda. Or she started to feel like she was losing Nick and the only way to get him back was to be the one in control again." Amanda thought about her own mother. "For people like her, losing control is a very scary thing. It's like they're losing their power."

"I feel so bad about it all." Jenny sniffed and wiped at her nose with the tissue again. "Like I'm partially responsible."

"Nonsense," Amanda said. "You can't feel that

way. Yolanda made her choices. Now she's got to live with the consequences."

"I know. But I still feel bad."

"It's because you're a decent human being. And also probably because your emotions are pretty close to the surface right now. That tends to happen with brides."

"Yeah," Jenny said. "I have no doubt that's part of it, too." She smiled, even though her eyes were liquid with tears. "You're pretty smart, you know that?"

Amanda laughed. "I have the benefit of years of experience. Now, show me what you've got and let's see how much of this wedding planning I can take off your shoulders."

Jenny opened up her tote bag and they got to work.

Forty-five minutes later, Amanda knew exactly what needed to be done. She'd taken notes on everything Jenny had shown her while keeping a list of what was done, what still needed doing, and what needed confirming.

Amanda wanted to reassure Jenny that they were in a good place. "You've done a great job. You really have. This is a tremendous amount of work. It's no wonder you've been stressed. But at this point, I can absolutely take over things and handle it in such a way that you won't need to do too much more except show up and say I do."

Jenny's brows rose. "For real?"

Amanda nodded. "Yes. I'm sure I'll have questions for you here and there, but ultimately, you've done so much of it already that it's just a matter of keeping on top of the various vendors to make sure it all comes together at the right time and place."

Jenny's eyes kind of glazed over as she stared at the binder of wedding plans. "I have nightmares about that. I really do. Just last night I dreamed that the flowers arrived and they were funeral flowers. Don't ask me how I knew that, but they were. I've had dreams about my dress being ruined, about everyone showing up in swimsuits, and about it snowing."

Amanda let out a soft laugh. "Dreaming about stuff like that ahead of the wedding is totally normal. But hopefully this last week and a half won't be so bad."

Jenny nodded. "I hope it won't be either. I have my dad coming in, you know. That's enough of a stressor as it is. Not so much for me, but for my mom."

Amanda put her hand on Jenny's shoulder. "Your

mom is a grown woman. She can handle herself. You don't need to worry about her."

"I can't help it. She's my mom."

"I know. And I get that. But it's all going to be fine. You'll see."

"I hope you're right."

Amanda looked over her list of notes. "If I need something or can't find anything, I'll be in touch. Otherwise, you can assume everything is perfect and on track. Okay? But you can call me whenever you want, too."

Jenny smiled. "Thank you." She leaned forward and hugged Amanda. "I feel better already. Now maybe I can concentrate on getting my actual work done."

Amanda got up and pushed her chair back around behind her desk. "You have any concerns, or think of anything else, just reach out."

Jenny rose. "I will. Thanks again."

Amanda just smiled as Jenny left. As soon as she was gone, Amanda sat down and started organizing the binder Jenny had turned over to her. It was a great distraction from thinking about the Hestons, something she hadn't been able to let go of.

First thing on her list was to go through Jenny's vendors and make sure everything was good with them. The day of the wedding was no time to find out the florist didn't have the pink roses you were hinging your entire color scheme on. Although Amanda didn't have those concerns about the florist Jenny was using. Mindy, from Key Largo Florist, had done all of the resort's weddings ever since the very first one. There was no way Mindy would let them down. Not with the amount of business Mother's was giving her.

Amanda called through the list, leaving a few voicemails for some where she identified herself as the wedding planning for the couple. She saved the last two, which were David, who was catering the wedding, because they were having it here on Compass Key, and Chantelle, who was making the cake for the same reason.

Those two she planned to go see in person. It had always been her way when she'd been planning weddings before. She found that in-person visits got better service than simple phone calls, but in this case, visiting the vendors on the mainland wasn't as easy. She also didn't expect David or Chantelle not to give her good service. It was really more of an excuse to visit.

She took a break, letting Carissa know to call if she was needed, then walked over to The Palms.

David was behind the line, giving prep instructions to the cooks. She waited until he was done. He gave her a nod. "Hi, Amanda. Have you got another wedding for me?"

She smiled. They'd done quite a few together now and he was getting used to her visits meaning just that. "No. I just wanted to see if everything was on track for Nick and Jenny's reception."

He went to his desk in the corner and logged onto the computer. He opened their file. "Here's the menu. All I need is the final head count but the beginning of next week is fine for that. The food won't be ordered until that point."

"Of course." She leaned in, double-checking the menu against what she'd seen in Jenny's binder. "Looks great. Thank you."

"No problem."

Next, she went over to Chantelle's station, where she was piping coffee-colored flourishes onto individual chocolate cakes. "Those look fantastic."

"Special for this evening. Chocolate mocha cake. They're sinful, if I do say so myself."

"I bet they are."

Chantelle stopped piping for a second, her smile bright. "You want to take one with you?"

"Oh, no. But thanks." Amanda laughed. "I need

to fit into my dress for the weddings. Which is why I'm here, actually. I just wanted to check that you were good to go for Nick and Jenny's cake."

Chantelle's brow furrowed. "Not really. I mean, this is the first I'm hearing about it. Not that they were getting married, but that they wanted me to make the cake."

"Uh-oh. Okay, Jenny must have thought she called you but didn't. I realize we're less than two weeks away, but can you do it?"

"How big of a cake are we talking about?"

"Right now the head count stands at forty-five. So not a huge wedding, but I know wedding cakes aren't something you can just throw together overnight."

"What kind of cake are they looking for? If it's not too fancy, I'm sure I can fit it in."

Amanda nodded. "Thank you. I'll go grab the planner and be right back to show you want they want."

She went straight to her office and flipped to the cake section in the binder. There were several pictures of cakes along with a note in Jenny's handwriting that just said, "Talk to Chantelle."

Apparently, Jenny had never gotten that far. Amanda wasn't worried. Brides forgot things all the time. Thankfully, Chantelle wasn't just any baker. She was part of the Mother's team.

Amanda had every confidence the cake would get done. In fact, she decided right then and there not to even tell Jenny what had happened.

The last thing Jenny needed was something else to worry about.

Chapter Eighteen

eigh Ann strolled the pathway toward Grant's studio. She hadn't told Grant about Paul kissing her. There didn't seem to be any need. For one thing, Grant had started coming to the fitness center to work out. If he knew, he might want to confront Paul. Even if Grant said something jokingly, Paul might not take it well.

For another thing, it was over and done with and not something she wanted to revisit. Paul had apologized when she'd explained that she was in a serious relationship and besides that the resort had a rule that clients were off-limits. That wasn't really a rule, but Leigh Ann thought that it ought to be.

It was clear that Paul had miscalculated and that he felt bad. Probably a little embarrassed, too. She'd seen it in his eyes and body language, so she'd done her best to reassure him that it was forgiven and forgotten and that she was flattered to think he was interested. It *was* flattering to think that a movie star like Paul found her attractive, but she wasn't so naïve as to think he wanted anything more than a vacation fling.

And besides, what else could she say? He was a paying guest who'd made a mistake. She didn't want him to cancel his sessions or leave the resort early. She'd offered to switch him over to Lars, the new male trainer she'd hired in January, but Paul had declined, saying if she was all right with them going forward, so was he.

She was. She liked Paul and she thought they worked well together. But if he tried anything like that again, they were done. Once could be forgiven. Twice? Not so much.

She stood at the entrance to Grant's studio with a smile on her face, thinking about how blessed she was to have a man like him in her life. She loved watching him at work, paintbrush in hand. He always had such a look of concentration on his face when he was creating.

He was in front of a canvas, as usual, but the painting on it was anything but his typical. Since Christmas, when he'd painted a mermaid portrait of singer and resort guest Lala Queen, he'd developed a new style, something very different from what he'd been doing.

Lala had insisted on pink in her painting. It was

her signature color, and the color of her hair. Grant hadn't wanted to do the painting at all, but Leigh Ann had talked him into it.

Lala had wanted the painting so much she'd been willing to pay Grant dearly for it with a fat check and a lot of social media mentions, which had blown up Grant's name recognition in a major way. His online store had crashed twice because of it, and he'd sold out of more prints than he'd had in stock. Since then, his gallery had gained several new employees to handle all the shipping and the increase in visitors.

To say the painting had been a worthwhile undertaking, despite not wanting to do it, was an understatement.

But the experience had also made him think about his work in a different way. About how color played a part in it. He'd always painted pictures that were a kind of magical realism. Sea goddesses who lived beneath the waves and ruled the creatures that made the ocean their home. But always in the colors that represented those things as they truly were.

Now, he'd welcomed in a new use of color, still creating the kinds of scenes he was known for but instead of the blues and greens of natural life, he added bold strokes of vibrant purples, brilliant yellows, fiery reds, exciting greens, intense oranges, and deep indigos.

To him, those colors were a new way of expressing emotion and feeling in his paintings and he was like a kid who'd been turned loose in a candy store. She'd never seen him so excited as she had these past few months.

He was as transformed as his artwork. If before his paintings had looked like a glimpse into a magical underwater world, they now looked like that same world seen through a kaleidoscope.

His work had become, in the words of Cheyanne, the young woman who managed Grant's galley, next level.

Not only had his first public painting in this style commanded an outrageous price at auction, but Grant had been interviewed by some big magazines, a couple of nationwide television shows, and even invited onto a late-night chat show.

The move into bold color had propelled him to new heights. He'd even hired Jenny to run a portion of his PR. Cheyanne took care of the gallery's social media accounts, which hadn't even existed before.

Grant Shoemaker had legitimately become a celebrity.

Hard to imagine. And yet, not. When she looked

at his work, it was harder to imagine why it had taken so long.

Of course, she was biased. She was his muse, after all. He'd painted her into several of his pictures. Then there was also the whole thing where she was madly in love with him. That tended to change a person's outlook.

She took a few steps in. "Am I disturbing you?"

With his eyes still on the canvas, he smiled. "You already know the answer to that question." He finished whatever he was doing and looked up. "Hi."

"Hi," she returned the greeting as she walked toward him. "How's it coming?"

"I'm happy with it. Quite a departure from what I'm used to, as you know, but nothing ventured, nothing gained." He stepped back, gaze tentative. "What do you think of *The Shark Sorceress* so far?"

Not only had he started using color in interesting ways, but he'd delved into slightly darker themes than in previous paintings, using the brilliant colors to lighten what might otherwise be a subject that would turn viewers off.

"Ohhh, that is so cool." Leigh Ann stared into the portal he'd created, at the world unveiled by his hand.

A woman, a sea goddess, stood at the entrance of

an underwater palace on a high cliff, a staff in one hand, the other thrust before her toward a sea that teemed with sharks, all of them circling. All of them obeying her.

The woman was merely a sketch, but already Leigh Ann could see the power in her form, the way she commanded attention.

Grant's eyes narrowed. "It's different, though. I know that."

"It's beautiful. And powerful." Leigh Ann looked over her shoulder at him. "It's amazing."

"It needs you." He smiled, clearly pleased with her assessment. "I know we have the wedding tomorrow and it's going to be a busy day, but how about the day after that? Can you sit for me?"

She nodded. "I'll give you all the free time I have."

"Thank you." He came up behind her and put his arms around her. "I couldn't do this without you, you know."

She smiled and leaned back into him. "That is very sweet of you to say, but it seems only fair to remind you that you were doing this long before I arrived on Compass Key."

"Not like this, though. The difference is night and day." He kissed her shoulder. "You're the one who got me to do the portrait for Lala. Left on my own, I never would have done that. It's changed so much for me. I owe you for that. For pushing me to be more. For giving me the kind of inspiration I'd needed for years."

"You're giving me too much credit." She turned in his arms so she could see him. "But I'm just as glad for having you in my life. I hope you know that. So long as you aren't saying all that to get out of our next workout."

He laughed. "No, I promise that's not it. I thought working out together was fun. Even if it did leave me feeling like an old man."

She'd talked him into lifting some weights with her. Paul's attempt at transformation had inspired her a little, so she'd decided to train heavier one day a week. Grant had joined in.

"Well, you don't look like an old man."

"Good thing that." He kissed her.

She wrapped her arms around his neck and as the kiss ended, she stared up at him. "Tomorrow will be a fun day, huh?"

He nodded. "It will be. Very fun."

She cut her eyes at him. "You sound like you know something I don't."

"I do. I know the location of the ceremony."

She sucked in a breath. "You do? And you haven't told me?"

He laughed. "I can't. I've been sworn to secrecy."

"Seriously? Not even Katie knows. Or does she and she's just keeping mum, too?"

He shook his head. "Not sure." Then he frowned and let go of her to put a hand on his chest. He exhaled hard, open-mouthed. "I think I've been on my feet too long. I feel a little short of breath."

He wobbled slightly and she grabbed his arm. Panic zipped through her belly. Her own heart started to beat faster. "Are you okay?"

Hand still on his chest, he winced and stumbled backwards toward his chair. "I...I don't think so."

Chapter Nineteen

"*I*t's not a date," Iris said, even as she smiled into her bathroom mirror. She'd taken extra care with her eyebrows, making sure they were penciled in just so. They'd gotten so thin over the years.

Vera put her hands on her hips. "Are you sure? You're wearing makeup. And I don't mean powder and rouge. Actual makeup. You haven't taken this much time getting ready since...since I don't know when."

"That's not true." Although, Iris thought, maybe it was. She waved a dismissive hand at her friend and housekeeper. "I wear makeup all the time. Besides, there's nothing wrong with wanting to look my best. And it's good practice for the wedding tomorrow."

"Nothing wrong with looking your best at all," Vera said, eyes sparkling. "Not when there's an eligible bachelor in the mix."

They only knew Emerson Hutch was eligible because that's what his Wikipedia page said about him. Not that Iris had really known what a Wikipedia page was, but Vera was well-informed about such things.

Iris applied a light coating of Honeysuckle to her lips, the pinky-coral color the perfect complement to her floral sundress and lightweight cardigan. She rolled her lips together to smooth the color out, then put the top back on the tube and looked at Vera in the mirror. "Don't you have work to do?"

"Nope." Vera grinned. "You look lovely. I'm sure he'll be instantly smitten."

Iris just rolled her eyes and shook her head. "That isn't my goal but thank you all the same."

A knock on the door turned both their heads.

"I'll get it," Vera said as she headed out of the room.

"Thank heavens for small favors." Iris grabbed her little raffia clutch, tucked her lipstick into it along with her phone and the pack of tissues it already held, then followed after Vera.

Katie was at the door. She smiled at Iris. "We're on our way to the restaurant. Just wanted to see if you'd like to walk with us. If you're ready."

"I am and I'd love to walk with you," Iris answered. "Don't you look beautiful." Katie was in a strapless black and white polka dot sundress with black sandals. The diamond necklace Iris had given her was around her neck, a nice match to the rock Owen had put on her finger. Katie looked radiant. And happy. Which was exactly how a woman should look on the eve of her wedding.

"Thank you. You look pretty fantastic yourself." She pursed her lips like she was trying not say anything else.

Iris ignored that to glance over her shoulder, one hand on the door handle. "See you later, Vera."

She was already settling down in front of the television. She gave Iris a wave. "Have a nice dinner."

Iris closed the door and followed Katie down to the path where the rest of her family awaited. They all said hello and she greeted them in return. She was glad to see Gage with Sophie. It made Iris feel less like the lone outsider, even if she did consider Katie family and vice-versa.

Emerson, dapper in tan trousers, a pink and white striped shirt, and straw fedora, appeared next to her. He smelled of a nice aftershave and soap. "Good evening, Iris. You sure look pretty."

She almost laughed at how good his words made her feel. "That's very kind of you, Emerson. You look rather smart yourself."

"Clothes make the man," he said.

She nodded. "They do indeed."

The comfortable small talk continued as they walked. He told her about the day he'd spent at Owen's, getting to meet first Katie's son and his family, and then, of course, Owen himself. Emerson had been given an extensive tour of Owen's property, which had impressed him, as had the man. He nodded ahead of them toward the billionaire. "He's got quite a head on his shoulders that one. Good thing, too, because Katie's no dummy."

"No, she's not," Iris agreed. "I wouldn't have passed on a portion of this place to her if she was."

"I guess not," Emerson said. He waggled his brows. "I like to think smarts run in the family."

She laughed. "Well, you're obviously a clever man. Takes talent and know how to be a working musician." She didn't tell him about looking him up online today with Vera's help. Even listened to some of his music, which she was pleased to have enjoyed.

"It definitely takes talent, but it takes perseverance, too. Lot of rejection in what I do. It either thickens your skin or kills your dream. Harsh, maybe, but true. Katie knows all about that, what with her being a writer."

Iris nodded. She had a great deal of respect for Katie's career. "She's inspired me, you know. I've been slowly writing up my memories and, bit by bit, she's turning them into a book for me."

"That is very exciting!"

She shrugged one shoulder. "I don't know if it is or not, but the girls have convinced me that visitors to the resort would be interested in the story behind this place, how it came about, my late husband's dream of it, all of that. I guess we'll see once it's done."

"I'll take a copy." He winked. "So long as you sign it for me."

He was so charming he made her feel like she was floating. It also lit a small fire under her to get more work done on her memoire. "I would be happy to sign one for you. Or trade you for one of your signed albums."

His brows went up, nearly disappearing under his hat. "You want one of those? I'll get you one, you bet."

Ever the gentleman, he made sure to hold the door for her as they went into her namesake restaurant.

Grace approached as the group gathered at the hostess stand. "Hi, everyone." She gave them a wave before gathering up menus. "I'm going to be taking special care of you all tonight."

"Grace, you don't have to do that," Katie said.

"Actually, I do," Grace said with a little chuckle. "I'll explain on the way."

She led them into the private room, speaking softly to Katie as they went. Katie looked concerned, nodded a few times, then gave Grace's arm a squeeze. Iris wasn't sure what was going on, but had no doubt she'd find out soon enough.

They all took seats at the long table. Emerson was at one end, Owen at the other, the rest of them in between. Iris was next to Emerson, with Sophie next to her. Across from them were Gage and Josh, Katie's son. Christy, the kids, and Katie were next to them. So many happy, beautiful faces.

There were already glasses of water on the table. Iris lifted hers. "Thank you, Katie and Owen and family, for letting me join you tonight. I feel blessed to be a part of such a wonderful celebration and I wish the bride and groom all the happiness life has to offer."

Everyone lifted their glasses to her toast and took a drink.

Emerson leaned toward her. "That was lovely. I feel blessed you're part of this, too."

She smiled at him. "You are quite the charmer, aren't you?"

He sat back slightly, lifting his chin, putting his hands flat on the table. "What I am is a man with too few years left looking at one of the loveliest creatures I've had the good fortune to meet, and I'm not about to be shy with my feelings now. Why should I? Unless you don't want me to, that is."

A strange breathlessness took hold of Iris, a feeling of being filled with light and opportunity, all accompanied by the sort of head-turning, anything-is-possible joy she hadn't felt since the fateful day Arthur Cotton had come into her life.

The feeling was reminiscent of the fizzy, bubbly incandescence of youthful infatuation. It was decadent and delicious.

It also wasn't something she'd imagined would fill her again. Not after Arthur. Not at this age. She opened her mouth to breathe more air into her lungs. This was heady stuff, and she had a decision to make.

But it didn't take long.

She slid her hand across the table until her fingertips touched Emerson's, a little spark of warmth jumping between them. "I want you to."

Chapter Twenty

*O*livia ended her call with Jenny, who'd filled her in on everything that had happened with Nick and Yolanda. Jenny had also thanked Olivia for talking to Nick.

Olivia had let out a sigh of relief. She wasn't sure her intervention would be welcomed, but she'd taken the risk and it had paid off. She was happy about that, to be sure.

Eddie was due around six for dinner, which wasn't going to be anything too fancy. She was roasting a chicken, steaming some broccoli, and for him, making a small amount of rice. She still tried to keep to a fairly low-carb, zero-sugar diet. It wasn't hard and the results, both in the way she looked and the way she felt, were definitely worth it.

She'd texted him earlier, just to say hi and that she'd see him later, but he had yet to text back. Not a big deal. If he had guests out on one of the boats, she didn't expect him to ignore them for her.

She rubbed the chicken down with butter, sprin-kled it liberally with her own mix of herbs, spices, and salt, then stuffed a cut-up lemon and some fresh rosemary in the cavity before popping it in the oven.

Funny how much she liked cooking now. She'd always been so tired after work in her life B.C.K., or Before Compass Key, as she thought of it, that fixing herself a meal was more of an effort than she wanted to put out.

Most usually, she'd resorted to frozen, pre-made meals eaten in front of the television. But now, in her life on the island, cooking was a lot more fun. For one thing, she wasn't exhausted after her day. For another, sharing most of her evenings with Eddie meant she had something to look forward to. And cooking for him, or with him, as the case was some-times, was really nice.

She went upstairs to the loft outside the master bedroom. She had a desk set up there that she used as a home office, but she'd recently added a couple sets of hand weights, a mat for stretching, and some heavy elastic bands for working out. On the wall near her desk, Eddie had helped her hang a television.

When it was too chilly to swim her laps, or she didn't feel like getting her suit on, she did a little exercise routine at home. Leigh Ann had helped her figure out what was best. Sometimes, Olivia did her routine in the morning before her shower.

The more she worked out and saw results, the more she liked doing it. She'd never have thought at her age that she could actually like the way her body looked. Amazing what a person could accomplish when she set her mind to it.

She changed out of her work clothes and into shorts and a T-shirt, then put on the news while she did her weights and stretching.

Watching the news wasn't high on her list of priorities, but living on the island occasionally made her forget there was a world beyond the crystal clear waters surrounding Mother's.

For the most part, it was all doom and gloom. Seeing the news just made her glad to live in the safe haven of the island.

She finished up on her mat, stretching out all the muscles she'd just used, then she took a quick shower and put on some comfy leggings and a soft sweatshirt. As she was coming down the stairs to check on the chicken, someone knocked at her door.

She opened it and smiled. "Hi, Eddie."

He didn't smile back. "Hi. Grant's in the hospital. They think he had a heart attack."

"What?" Olivia put her hand to her throat. "Is he okay?"

"He seems stable, but they're running tests. It's why I didn't text. I was taking him and Leigh Ann over there. He collapsed in the studio and she called Nick, then me, and we got him over there as soon as we could."

Olivia felt awful but she knew that didn't compare to what Leigh Ann must be feeling. "Is Leigh Ann still at the hospital?"

"Yes. Do you want to go?"

"I do. But first I'm going to text her and see if she needs anything." Olivia stepped out of the doorway. "Come in."

He came through, closing the door behind him. "Smells good in here."

"That's the chicken I was making for dinner." She texted as she talked. *Just heard about Grant. I'm so sorry. What do you need? I'll bring it over.* She hit Send. "Why didn't Leigh Ann send us a text? Too much going on?"

"I'm sure." He shrugged. "I also think she didn't want to text until she knew Grant was going to be okay. She was very upset."

"I would have been, too." Olivia shook her head. "How scary for both of them."

He nodded. "Grant was pretty shaken up. He's not a guy who gets frightened easily, but he definitely was. I think it made him feel better having Nick along."

"I'm so glad Nick is here now. Having a doctor on the island makes such a difference. Not that Peter didn't do a great job as a paramedic, but..."

"I know," Eddie said. "It's not exactly the same."

Olivia's phone buzzed. She checked the screen and read Leigh Ann's answer.

Thank you. I would love a jacket or a sweatshirt. The hospital is freezing.

"That was Leigh Ann," she told Eddie. "She wants a jacket or sweatshirt because it's cold over there. I'll bring her one of each and let her decide."

The oven timer went off.

Eddie glanced over. "Does that mean the chicken's done?"

She nodded.

"I'll get it out. You get the stuff for Leigh Ann."

"Okay." She left him to do that as she ran upstairs and grabbed a sweatshirt and a zip-up fleece jacket. She folded them both and stuck them in a tote bag along with an extra phone charger that she knew would work on Leigh Ann's phone, since they had the same kind. She looked around the room, trying to think of anything else her friend might need.

If there was anything, she'd happily run to the nearest store to get it.

Olivia went back downstairs. Eddie had the chicken out of the oven and into a glass storage container, covered in tinfoil, since the bird was just slightly too big for the top to go on. He put it in the fridge. "Ready?"

"Yes. Thanks for doing that." It was probably a little too hot to go into the fridge, but there was no other choice.

They were both quiet on the ride over and on the way into the hospital, they held hands. Leigh Ann had just almost experienced one of Olivia's worst fears. Thankfully, Grant was stable. But the thought that the person you loved could be so suddenly taken from you...that terrified Olivia.

They got Grant's room number and went on up.

Leigh Ann stood as they entered the room. Olivia gave her a big hug, holding her close, and smiled at Grant. "How are you doing?"

Grant nodded. "I'm all right. It wasn't a heart attack, they don't think. But they don't know what it was yet."

Eddie shook Grant's hand. "Glad to hear it wasn't your heart."

"Me, too," Grant said.

Olivia handed Leigh Ann the duffel bag. "I brought you a jacket and a sweatshirt. Take your pick."

"Thanks." Leigh Ann unzipped the bag and dug out the sweatshirt. "I'm so cold I might put both of them on. Oh! You brought me a phone charger. That was so thoughtful. Thank you. I can definitely use that."

"You're welcome."

She pulled on the sweatshirt, then got her phone plugged in.

They all sat and chatted about nothing in particular, like they were dancing around the reason Grant was here, but Olivia understood. Both he and Leigh Ann probably needed a break from thinking about what might have happened.

Eddie leaned forward. "Do you think you'll be able to make it to the wedding tomorrow?"

Grant nodded. "They're going to keep me overnight, then run one more test in the morning. If that shows no sign of heart attack, which I'm sure it won't, then I'll be discharged."

Leigh Ann smiled. "I think you'll be discharged

either way. And we don't have to be at the dock until three. We should be fine to make the wedding."

Olivia was relieved. "Good. I want us all to be together."

"Me, too," Leigh Ann said.

After a quick knock, the door opened and Nick walked in, followed by an older woman in scrubs and a lab coat.

Leigh Ann got to her feet. "Dr. Allessa." She glanced at Olivia. "Dr. Allessa is the cardiologist."

The older woman gave them all a reassuring smile as she stood beside Grant's bed. "I've looked at all the test results and everything the scans could show me and I believe you have costochondritis."

Leigh Ann sank back down into her chair. "That doesn't sound good."

Nick shook his head. "It's not that bad."

Dr. Allessa spoke. "Costochondritis is an inflammation of the cartilage where the ribs and sternum meet. There are a lot of things that can cause it. Even a hard cough or moving furniture can do it."

Grant let out a sigh. "Or, say, lifting weights with your girlfriend who's a beast in the gym?"

Dr. Allessa laughed. "That could definitely do it. We're going to get you on some ibuprofen. By morning, you should feel a lot better."

Leigh Ann groaned and put her face in her hands. "I can't believe this is because we worked out."

Nick snorted. "Hey, this was a good outcome."

Leigh Ann looked up. "Yes, it was." She got up again and went to Grant's bedside. "I'm so glad you're okay. I'm sorry I pushed you so hard."

He laughed. "Don't be sorry. I'm obviously in worse shape than I thought. But maybe next time we'll go a little lighter, huh?"

"Yeah, for sure." Leigh Ann exhaled.

"All right," Dr. Allessa said. "You folks have a good night."

Olivia got up and went to Leigh Ann's side as the doctor left. Leigh Ann looked at Nick. "Still a good thing you were there."

He smiled. "I'm glad I was. And honestly, this was a learning experience for me. I've never had a case of chest pains that turned out to be costochondritis. But if you guys don't need me anymore, I think I'll head back with Eddie and Olivia."

Leigh Ann bent to give Grant a kiss.

Olivia smiled at Nick. "We'd be happy to take you home."

Leigh Ann straightened and hugged Olivia. "Thanks for coming." She looked at Eddie. "Both of you. And listen, don't say anything about what happened, okay? I don't want anyone freaking out. We'll tell everyone in person tomorrow. Or maybe sometime after the wedding." She took Grant's hand. "When we can laugh about it."

Eddie stood, nodding. He clapped Grant on the shoulder. "Not a word, *amigo*."

"Thanks," Grant said.

Olivia and Eddie said goodbye and left with Nick. As they walked down the hall, Eddie took Olivia's hand and looked at her. "I told you working out was dangerous."

She just laughed and kissed him.

Chapter Twenty-one

Grace accepted hugs from Katie, Owen, and Iris as they got ready to leave the restaurant.

"Outstanding meal," Owen said.

"Divine," Iris said, then her gaze immediately shifted back to Katie's uncle, who seemed glued to her side.

"Thank you for taking care of us." Katie held onto Grace's hands for an extra second. "That was above and beyond. I appreciate it so much. Especially since we didn't do the whole rehearsal dinner thing."

"Well, I had help. It's not like I had to do it on my own." Two of the food runners had stepped in to assist Grace and make sure the large party was well taken care of. Grace was going to divide Katie's generous tip between them. She didn't need any of it.

What she needed was a long soak in a hot bath with a heaping pile of bubbles.

Katie smiled. "See you tomorrow."

"You bet," Grace said. "Big day. I can't wait."

Katie sighed and looked dreamily at Owen. "Me either."

Grace grinned and waved goodbye to them all. One of the busboys, Diego, approached her. "Okay to clean the room now?"

She nodded. "Yes. Thank you."

"You got it, Miss Grace."

She thought about going to help clean for maybe two seconds, then decided she'd done enough. She went to cash herself out and pull the tip so she could split it between Hannah and James, the two food runners. They'd tip out from that to the busboys. After that was done, she went into the kitchen to say goodnight to her husband, glad he'd decided to work at Iris's this evening.

David had his back to her, speaking to one of the line cooks, but he smiled when he turned around and saw her. "How did it go?"

"Great. They loved everything. It was nice of you to send those extra apps out."

"Those stuffed mushrooms are easy to whip up and always a crowd pleaser. I was happy to do it." He tipped his head. "Is it okay if I say you look tired?"

She snorted softly. "It is, because I am. Being a

floor manager is one thing. Waiting on a big party is completely another."

"Go home and relax. You've earned it. I'll be right behind you in a couple hours."

"I might be asleep by then." She untied her apron and tossed it in the used linens bin by the door.

"That's okay."

She kissed her fingers, then blew the kiss to him through the stainless-steel shelves where ready-to-be-served plates were placed. "See you at home."

"Bye, honey."

She took off, waving to the other employees as she went. She stepped outside, inhaling the night air with its hints of woodsmoke, salt, and pool water. Her stomach growled for food, spurred on by the pizza aroma from next door.

But she had food at the bungalow and no desire to wait in line at Castaways. She strolled home, the fresh air giving her a boost of new energy. Not enough that she was going to change her mind about going to bed, but enough that she'd be able to get something to eat, take a bath, then fall asleep with some silly television program droning in the background.

Grace considered herself a pretty good judge of

character, a better-than-average reader of body language, and a close listener. If she'd learned anything this evening, it was that Iris was about to have an epic romance.

The very thought made her smile. Iris deserved to find love again. And if this wasn't love exactly, then she at least deserved to have a little fun. Katie's uncle was cool guy. Handsome. Well-dressed. Obviously had a sense of humor. And clearly liked Iris, something he didn't seem shy about showing.

Grace hoped whatever happened between them was mutual and fun and no hearts were broken. She couldn't take a broken-hearted Iris. She loved the dear old woman too much.

She climbed the bungalow steps, let herself into the place, grabbed an apple muffin off the counter, and went straight upstairs to run a bath, adding a big glug of coconut bath bubbles. She finished the muffin as she stripped out of her uniform of black pants and lavender shirt embroidered with the name Iris's over the left chest and tossed them in the hamper.

Her dress for the wedding tomorrow, along with David's suit and shirt, were hooked by their hangers to the closet door.

Tomorrow was going to be an amazing day. She

clipped her hair up, put her phone on the edge of the tub, then slid into the hot, bubbly, coconut-scented water and closed her eyes. This was just what she needed, no doubt.

The water was piping hot and completely soothing. She could feel the tiredness disappearing, replaced by a blissful state of relaxation.

Until her phone buzzed, nearly vibrating itself into the tub. She grabbed it before that happened. The screen showed a group message from Katie.

If you're up and around, come join us at the Parrot Lounge. My uncle is going to play the piano! The text was followed by three emojis: a smiley face, a heart, and a music note.

Grace snapped a picture of her toes, nearly hidden by bubbles, and sent the pic along with a short note. *Too late!*

Still, Grace regretted not being able to go. Seeing Katie's uncle do what he did best would have been fun.

But Grace would have plenty of fun tomorrow.

🌴 🌴 🌴

Katie stood outside the Parrot Lounge, checking her replies. "Looks like everyone else is tied up or already in for the night. No worries, though. I'll take a little video and send it." She hooked her arm through Iris's. "Let's go on in. What a good idea you had."

Iris smiled. "I don't know why I didn't think of it sooner. This piano doesn't get played enough as it is."

There were a few guests in the lounge. Katie hoped they didn't mind a little impromptu show. If they did, well...too bad.

Uncle Hutch made a big show of lacing his fingers together and stretching them out. "I hope I remember how."

They all laughed. All of them except Christy and Josh, who'd taken the kids back to the guest house at Owen's, although Josh had promised to returned once the kids were tucked in, eager to see his great-uncle's musical talents.

Katie's concerns about the other guests possibly not enjoying a little live music were made pointless by Iris's announcement.

"Ladies and gentlemen, I'm Iris Cotton, founder of this resort, and I want you to know you're in for a special treat this evening. Mother's has with us one of the best jazz piano players in the world."

Katie rolled her lips in to keep from laughing.

Iris's lack of subtlety had no shame.

Iris went on. "He's left New Orleans to visit us here and I couldn't be happier that he's decided to grace us with his talents. It is my pleasure to introduce the legendary Emerson Hutch."

The small crowd applauded, and Uncle Hutch looked like he was glowing from within as he bowed and took a seat at the piano.

He placed his hands on the keys and ran the scales up and down. Then he winked at Katie, or possibly Iris, who was right next to her, and started to play for real. His fingers danced across the keyboard, sending a rollicking ragtime number out with the kind of energy that made him seem like a man of thirty or forty.

Although the small crowd had applauded after Iris's introduction, it appeared they'd done so out of politeness, looking fairly indifferent. Until now. *Now* the guests in attendance had all turned to face the piano. Heads were nodding, feet were tapping, and there were smiles on almost all the faces, the bartender included.

Iris was grinning and clapping along. Owen was bobbing his head. Sophie and Gage were side by side, hands entwined, which Katie thought was a very good sign.

A couple of guests on the other side of the lounge moved a table and two chairs out of the way and started to dance.

When the song came to an end, the applause was twice as loud as the first round and accompanied by shouts for more.

Uncle Hutch dove right into another one with the same amount of enthusiasm and gusto. Katie got her phone out to shoot a video and she realized in that moment how much she'd missed out on without him in her life. She and Sophie had been so wrapped up in work that all they'd ever done was talk about visiting him. They'd never actually done it.

How was she supposed to go another five years without seeing him? What if the worst happened and there wasn't that much time left?

For all the joy in her heart, there was a new feeling there, too. A kind of desperate longing to preserve this moment. To make it last. To make it more than a moment. To make it permanent.

Iris leaned in toward Katie. "What do you think it would take to get your uncle to stay?"

Katie inhaled at the question. Had Iris read her mind? "I was just wondering the same thing."

Chapter Twenty-two

*A*manda bit her bottom lip as she stood in the middle of Duke's living room. "We could get into a lot of trouble for this."

"You're an owner, I'm an employee," Duke said. "We have every right to be in their bungalow. And if we need an excuse, we'll just say there was a report of someone trying to get in through the rear sliders."

"A possible break-in doesn't make the resort look good," Amanda said.

He nodded. "No, you're right. I'll grab my toolbox and bring it along. We'll say the compressor was making a funny noise. Considering I just had to replace one, that's not far off."

"That explains the presence of the head of maintenance, but not me."

He grinned at her. "Maybe you're the one who heard it? Maybe you're there as a chaperone. Maybe it's just resort policy that after-hours maintenance calls are attended by an owner?"

She shot him a look. "I don't like this."

Duke nodded. "I know, but I'm telling you, I heard them talking and it didn't sound good."

"Tell me what you thought you heard again?"

"He said something about time running out and she said something like she was sure it was going to happen tomorrow and then he said, 'Well, we'd better find out for sure because if we miss it, we're both getting fired.'" Duke shrugged. "Sounded to me like they weren't here for a vacation after all."

"No, it doesn't." She sighed. "I knew the Hestons were trouble."

"Which is why I was doing recon in the first place."

She almost laughed. He was clearly enjoying this. "Recon?"

"Yes."

"You mean eavesdropping."

"Same thing." He smirked as he got a toolbox out of the coat closet. She was pretty sure that wasn't his main toolbox. Probably just one he kept around for small repairs. "Hey, if they're going to have conversations on their back deck while I'm working next door, it's not my fault if I overhear."

"No, I guess not."

He shifted his grip on the toolbox and took her hand. "I know you're nervous about this, but they went to dinner on the mainland. Lorenzo promised he'd text me when he was bringing them back."

Lorenzo was the newest boat captain.

"Okay. Let's go. I hope we're both wrong about them."

"So do I."

They went out, Duke locked the door and they started down the path toward the guest bungalows. Amanda's master keycard felt like a ten-pound weight in her pocket, but she couldn't shake the feeling she'd had since the Hestons had arrived. All because of his watch and his attitude. *His watch.* She grabbed Duke's arm. "I know what it was about that Rolex that made me think something was up."

"What?"

"The second hand. It didn't sweep. It ticked. Rolexes don't do that, do they?"

"Nope. So it was a fake."

"I guess." She shook her head. "Why? So he'd look wealthier than he really is? If you can afford to stay here, what else matters?"

"I don't know. Do you think her purse was real? You said it was expensive."

"You know, I have no idea now. I know fakes are common. I guess it might have been, too. But again, why bother?"

"I guess they really wanted to look like they belong? Like they fit in here?"

"Which implies they don't." Amanda didn't like that idea at all. "And if that's true, why don't they belong? What are they here for if not a vacation?"

"Let's hope we can find out. Are there any other celebrities staying here right now? Anyone who might be a target of some kind?"

"There are almost always celebrities here. Paul De Luca is here now." Amanda gasped. "And according to Leigh Ann, he's here for the sole purpose of losing weight and building muscle for some new role that's supposed to take his career to the next level." She looked at Duke. "Do you think these two could be paparazzi trying to get the scoop on that?"

"Anything's possible. Didn't you say the guy was a freelance journalist?" Duke slowed as they approached the Hestons' bungalow.

"That's what I found out about him online. He's supposedly writing a book, but I'm starting to think you're right. These two could absolutely be paparazzi digging for a story. And pictures. If there's camera equipment in that bungalow, that could be a pretty big clue."

She and Duke went up the steps. Duke looked around. "There's no one nearby."

"Good." Amanda dug the key from her pocket. Her nerves were jangling. She unlocked the door, and they slipped inside. She left the lights off.

Duke reached over and flipped them on. "Don't freak out. Just act like we're here for a valid reason. Which we are. But you know what I mean. Anyway, maintenance wouldn't make a call in the dark."

"Right." She exhaled. "Okay. Let's do this quickly."

"I'll take the bedroom."

"Good." She looked around the living room. There was a laptop on the coffee table in front of the couch. Next to the laptop was a notebook, a pen, and an iPad. She wasn't going to mess with the electronics, but the notebook was fair game.

She took a good look at how it was positioned next to the laptop before picking it up. She wanted to be sure she put it back in the same spot. She reached for it, her heart pounding. But then she reminded herself how much was at stake here. If the Hestons really were paparazzi after Paul De Luca, and they got a story and pictures out, Mother's reputation as a safe place for the rich and famous to relax would be tarnished for a long time to come.

It would take a heck of a lot more than Jenny's PR skills to recover from a thing like that.

Amanda grabbed the notebook and flipped to the first page. It was all notes about the Hestons' travel arrangements. Flight times, confirmation numbers, stuff like that. Nothing useful.

She went through the next few pages and found names and numbers. Just first names, so they didn't mean a whole lot. But a few of the numbers were Florida area codes. Why would the Hestons have those when they were from L.A.?

She took her phone out and snapped a picture of those. She could research them later, if need be.

Duke stuck his head out of the bedroom. "Find anything yet?"

"Nothing really. Still looking. You?"

He held up a black bag. "Camera equipment."

She made a face. "It might not mean anything, but then again... If it's digital, can you look at any of the pictures that have been taken? That might tell us."

He unzipped the bag, pulled out the camera, turned it on and scanned back through the photos on the memory card. "Just normal vacation pics. The marina, the beach, the room. Stuff like that."

"None of them together? Any of Paul?"

He shook his head. "No to both of those. None of either of the Hestons. But maybe they took all of those on their phones."

"Maybe. I don't know if it means anything."

"Me either." He turned the camera off and put it back in the bag. "Back to looking." But he stayed at the door, jerking his chin at the laptop. "You going to turn that thing on?"

She shook her head. "No. It's probably password protected and it might be set up to take a picture of anyone who tries to get into it. That's the last thing I want."

"Good point." With a grumpy sigh, he went back into the bedroom.

She turned through a few more pages of the notebook. She found something that stopped her. At first she thought it was more travel info. But no, that's not exactly what it was. It was a boat reservation. A charter. And it wasn't through the resort's marina, but it *was* for tomorrow.

"Duke?"

He came back out. "Find something?"

"I found a reservation for a charter boat for tomorrow. A boat named *Skyfish*. The name Captain Iggy Alford is next to it. Mean anything to you?"

Duke snorted. "Yeah, actually. He's out of Bluewater. And I know him because he's a friend of my dad's. They fish together. I've been out with them. Small world. But what does that mean to us?"

"I don't know, but they've booked the boat for all day tomorrow." She glanced from the notebook to him. "Don't you think it's weird that they booked an outside company when they could have gotten Nico or Eddie or Lorenzo?"

"Maybe." He thought about it for a second. "But maybe they didn't know they could get a boat through the resort."

"I don't buy that. It's pretty well covered on the website how many different experiences we offer through the marina."

"Okay, so maybe they booked it, but cancelled?"

"Could be. Does your dad know this guy well enough to find out?"

"Yes, but actually, I have his number, too." Duke pulled his phone out and headed for the bedroom again. "I'll call him right now."

"Thanks." But what did it mean? Why would they book an off-island boat for the whole day? That wouldn't be cheap. Chartering the boat had to be related to whatever Duke had overhead the Hestons talking about. It was no coincidence that the events were on the same day.

A few minutes later, Duke came back. "The *Skyfish* is picking the Hestons up at our marina tomorrow at nine. Iggy says they didn't ask to go anywhere, just to tour them around the place and stand by for further instructions."

"That's not weird at all." She turned a few more pages and saw a note that made her jaw fall open. She closed it and shook her head. "They're not here for Paul."

"No?" Duke walked over.

She turned the notebook around so he could see the bold letters that spelled out, "Monk Wedding." "They're here for Owen and Katie."

Chapter Twenty-three

*L*eigh Ann yawned and looked at the time on her phone. A little after six a.m., so it was no wonder she was awake. Sleeping on the small couch in Grant's hospital room hadn't exactly been restful, but she didn't care. It had been worth an uncomfortable night to be with him.

There were other messages on her phone. Two of them were group messages. She pulled the first one up and squinted at the screen. She'd forgotten her reading glasses, but it looked like it was from what she called the Big Group that included all four of her sorority sisters plus Iris and Vera. That message read, *Happy Wedding Day to Owen and Katie!* and was from Iris.

The second message was from Amanda and had been sent to Leigh Ann, Olivia, and Grace. No Katie, which was odd. Maybe something about the wedding that Amanda didn't want Katie to know?

Leigh Ann opened it and read.

We have a problem. There are paparazzi on the island. They're in Bungalow 19. The Hestons. I'll explain how I know later. They're here for the wedding. What do we do? I've said nothing to Katie or Owen.

Leigh Ann read the message twice to be sure she understood it correctly. The nerve. Immediately, her need to protect her friend kicked in. She typed a fast answer, her gut reaction borne out of anger. *We stop them, that's what we do.*

But how? came Amanda's quick reply.

Olivia chimed in next. *We have to figure something out. Katie will lose it.*

Which is why, Amanda said, *I've left her off this loop.*

Leigh Ann frowned at her screen.

"What's wrong?"

She looked up. Grant was awake. She smiled at him. "Good morning, handsome."

"Morning, beautiful." He tipped his head. "Now are you going to tell me what's wrong?"

She let out a long sigh. "Amanda found out there are paparazzi on the island, masquerading as guests. And they're here for the specific purpose of getting pics of Owen and Katie's wedding."

He grimaced. "Not good. Not good at all. Everything Owen's done has been to shut that down."

"Does anyone besides you know the location of the ceremony? Or could they have found out?"

He shook his head. "Besides me, Owen, and Gage, I don't think so. I don't know how they could. It's all been done very secretively. Everyone else involved has signed an NDA and they know how serious Owen is about all of this."

She tried to think. "Then maybe these paparazzi don't know either but they're hoping to figure it out in time to get pictures. I need to text Amanda and find out more."

"I should let Owen know what's going on."

Leigh Ann grimaced. "Can you swear him to secrecy so that Katie doesn't find out?"

"Trust me," Grant said. "I don't think he wants that any more than you do. But I will." He looked around. "Where is my phone?"

"It's with your clothes. Hang on, I'll get it." She got up, grabbed his phone, handed it to him, then went back to the couch.

Her fingers flew over her phone's touch screen. *How much do these paps know? Time? Location? Grant is telling Owen but swearing him to secrecy.*

She looked up. Grant had the phone to his ear. "Good wedding morning to you." He smiled. "I'm sure it will be." His smile disappeared. "Listen, I have some news that you can't tell Katie about. Leigh Ann just told me that there are paparazzi at the resort posing as guests. Somehow, they got wind of the wedding."

Grant listened a second, then shook his head. "Don't know that yet. I'll keep you posted. Okay. You're welcome."

He hung up. "Owen won't say a word to Katie or anyone else, but he is going to let Gage know."

A moment later, Leigh Ann's phone vibrated with an incoming call. Owen. She answered. "Hi. Sorry about all this."

"Thanks. I need some more information. How do you know there are paparazzi?"

"Amanda found out. I don't know how."

"Do you think she'd mind if I called her? I have to shut this down. I cannot have anything ruining this day for Katie."

"Absolutely, I get it. Call her. She won't mind at all."

"Great, thanks. See you soon."

"You got it." She hung up right as a nurse came in.

She smiled at both of them. "I just need to draw some blood for one last test and if that's all clear, we're going to get you out of here."

Grant stuck his arm out. "It can't happen soon enough. We have a wedding to get to."

As it happened, it was nearly four hours later when they actually got back to Leigh Ann's bungalow. Thankfully, Grant had brought his suit for the wedding over the previous day. And since Leigh Ann had scheduled all of her clients that day with other trainers, there wasn't too much for them to do.

He went straight to the kitchen once he was inside. "I don't know about you, but I'm starving."

"So am I." Neither of them had eaten anything at the hospital.

He started pulling things out of the fridge. "I'm thinking omelets with whatever you've got to go in them."

She joined him. "And how about some home fries? I've got a couple of redskin potatoes. I could dice them up fine with a little onion."

"My mouth is already watering. We need to get some coffee going, too."

"I'm on it." She slanted her eyes at him. "Shouldn't you be resting? All things considered?"

"*No.*" He smiled. "I'm just sore from working out, remember? That was confirmed this morning. And the ibuprofen they gave me is already doing its job. I feel great. Starving, but great."

She smiled. "Okay."

They went to work on breakfast. She got the

coffee going, then started the potatoes sizzling in some olive oil. She was about to clean up when her phone vibrated with a call from Amanda. The texts had been flying fast and furious all morning, so she could only imagine what was going on now. She walked into the living room as she answered. "Hey. How's Operation Secret Wedding going?" Olivia had come up with that.

Amanda laughed. "I think pretty well. I'll tell you what, Owen doesn't fool around when it comes to stuff like this."

"Why? What happened?"

"Well, as you know, the Hestons had a charter boat reserved today, apparently to scope out Owen's place for photos."

"Right." Amanda had explained earlier how she and Duke had visited the Hestons' bungalow and found out everything.

"Duke knew Iggy, the captain of the boat they had reserved. The guy's an old friend of his dad's. Anyway, Duke connected Owen with Iggy and apparently, Owen is paying the man twice what the Hestons were to keep them away from the location of the ceremony."

A slow smile spread across Leigh Ann's face. "I

have to say that doesn't surprise me at all. Go, Owen."

"But we still have a problem on our hands."

"Oh?" Leigh Ann sat on the couch. "What is it?"

Amanda sighed. "I know none of us tipped anyone off about the wedding or its location because, honestly, we have no clue where it's going to be. And we've been quiet about the wedding, too. As we promised we'd be."

Leigh Ann looked toward the kitchen where Grant was still working on breakfast. "Right."

"And we know Owen, Gage, or Grant wouldn't have said anything."

"You know he knows?"

"Yes. Owen told me."

"Then how do you think the Hestons found out there even was a wedding?"

Amanda groaned softly. "Simple. We weren't as quiet as we should have been. I think we talked about it on the island and we were overheard. Somehow, word got out."

"Hmm." Leigh Ann squinted in thought. "You think the leak came from a guest?"

"No." Amanda's voice held an edge of anger. "I think it came from a resort employee."

Chapter Twenty-four

Olivia finally put her phone down on the little table next to her recliner, where she was camped out with her laptop working from home until it was time to get ready for the wedding.

Her head was spinning from all the texts flying back and forth. She'd just gotten off the phone with Amanda, who'd just gotten off the phone with Leigh Ann and was now calling Grace to give her the latest.

They had a rotten egg to deal with. Possibly. If an employee had actually tipped off the paparazzi in hopes of a big payday, it was up to management to ferret that person out and fire them. A thing like that could kill the resort's reputation. And business.

Which was exactly why employees signed a contract stating that they would respect the privacy of the resort's guests. It was explicit that guests at Mother's were not to be asked for autographs or selfies, nor were employees permitted to talk about them on social media. If a guest wanted to post that they were at Mother's, that was their business.

No one else's.

Olivia's best thought about how to find an employee who might have traded information for money was to keep an eye on all of them and see if someone showed up with a big-ticket item, or talked about buying something expensive, because if money wasn't the motivation behind such an act, she wasn't sure what else would be.

If she could have a look at all of the employee bank accounts, that would be an easy way to narrow down the list of possible suspects. A big influx of cash would send up a giant red flag. But accessing their bank accounts was illegal and an invasion of privacy.

Kind of like what Amanda and Duke had done, except what they'd done wasn't illegal. Amanda was an owner and had every right to enter a property on the island. Also, if she and Duke hadn't done some digging, none of them would know what the Hestons were really up to. Owen and Katie would once again be thrust into the public eye, open to the scrutiny of anyone with access to the internet.

It wasn't fair. People deserved their privacy, especially on a day like their wedding.

Olivia understood that with celebrity came some

tradeoffs. But neither Katie nor Owen had asked for that fame. In fact, Katie had done her best to avoid it by not even writing under her real name.

Again, Olivia shook her head at the unfairness of it. She was mad about the whole thing and because Eddie was working this morning, didn't have him to talk to about it. She'd been talking to the girls all morning. They already knew how she felt, because they all felt that way, too.

At least Owen had been able to intervene. Sometimes money really did buy happiness. Or at least, in this case, a little privacy.

But what if the Hestons weren't the only paparazzi who knew? What if there was a second pair of them?

She groaned. She couldn't think about the possibilities or she'd make herself crazy. Her phone buzzed.

She checked the screen expecting to see another group text, but it was from Jenny.

On my way over.

Olivia smiled. That was a nice surprise. *Door's open. Come on in.*

Jenny showed up a few minutes later, walking right in as Olivia had said to do. "Hi, Mom."

"Hi, honey. How are you?"

"Excited for the wedding. And weirdly nervous for Katie and Owen. Is that strange? I'm probably channeling my own stuff into today." She took a seat on the couch.

"Are you still nervous about your own wedding?"

"You know, not really. I'm surprised how much it helps to have Amanda overseeing everything." She shook her head. "I should have gone to her much, much sooner. Lesson learned. Not that I'm ever getting married again."

"Right," Olivia said. She was not about to tell Jenny what had transpired overnight. Although... Jenny was handling Katie and Owen's PR. Maybe Olivia should tell her. "If I tell you something, can you swear to keep it a secret from Katie?"

Jenny's brow furrowed. "I don't know if I can or not. It kind of depends what it is."

Olivia shook her head. "Then I can't tell you. Katie doesn't need anything to ruin this day for her."

"Is it a wedding thing?"

"Yes. Mostly."

"Does Owen know?"

"He does. And he's on board with keeping Katie in the dark. For now."

Jenny pursed her lips and went silent for a couple of seconds. "Then I guess I can keep it zipped up, too. What's going on?"

Olivia explained everything that Amanda had uncovered. The more she talked, the more Jenny's jaw dropped.

She blinked a few times. "That has to have been an employee. I know this is a big ask, but do you think we could come up with a list of the employees most likely to have overheard something?"

Olivia gave her a skeptical look. "That's a big list."

"Yeah, I figured. That's why I was just wondering if there was any way to eliminate some of them."

"Can I ask why you want that information?"

"Because with those names, I can find their social media accounts. And from there, I can dig further and see if any of them said or posted anything that might be incriminating."

Olivia's brows shot up. "That is a really good idea." She tapped a few keys on the laptop and brought up her master employee list. She stared at it. "Mother's employs a *lot* of people. You really want to do this?"

"We're talking about Katie and Owen here. And

the good name of this place. Yes," Jenny said. "For all this place has given me, I want to do this."

"Okay, but I don't know where to start."

"Well..." Jenny tapped her finger against her chin. "Do you think it's more likely to be a new hire? Or someone who's been here a while?"

Olivia frowned. "I have no idea. It could be a new hire who has no real loyalty to us yet. Or someone who's been here a while and is disgruntled for some reason?"

"Do you know of anyone who isn't happy, then?"

She thought hard. "To be honest, no. We pay well, have great benefits, and generally go out of our way to keep employees happy."

"How about this—let's eliminate, for now, anyone who lives on the property. I find it hard to believe someone would risk the roof over their head for something like this. I could be wrong, but it's a place to start."

"Agreed," Olivia said.

They worked for about an hour, going through the names and sorting them into different lists: Likely, Possibles, and Unlikely. There was nothing scientific about it. Just Olivia's own personal experience and their best guesses.

At the end of the hour, they had thirty names on

the Likely list. Jenny took that back to her place to start digging.

Olivia hoped she found something, but at the same time, she also hoped it was a dead end.

She hated to think that a resort employee was behind this.

Chapter Twenty-five

*G*race sprayed a little more hairspray on, then went back to work on her makeup. She was excited for the wedding but also excited to attend an event with David. They didn't get to do much of that. And a wedding was extra fun. Especially when the groom was a billionaire, and the budget was unlimited. Plus, they were dressed up. That just took everything up a notch.

The invites had said Tropical Formal. She hadn't been entirely sure what that meant but since they were being picked up by boat, she figured that meant dressy, but not so dressy it didn't work for the kind of island life they were all used to.

Her dress was a beautiful black floral with cap sleeves and a flowy skirt. She was pairing it with sparkly black sandals. David was wearing a light-weight gray suit with an almost matching black floral tie. It had taken no small amount of internet searching to find that tie and she was pretty pleased with how coordinated they looked.

She finished her makeup and came out of the

bathroom to see him checking himself out in the mirror.

He shook his head. "This feels weird."

She leaned on the bathroom door, floored by how handsome he was. "But you look so hot."

He grinned. "Yeah?"

She exhaled as she nodded. "Yeah."

He held his hand out to her, pulling her toward him when she took it. "You don't look so bad, either."

"Thanks." She leaned up to kiss him. "I suppose we should head to the marina."

He sighed happily. "I suppose we should."

She grabbed her little black purse, which held a card for the couple, while he got the keys, and they headed out. In lieu of presents, Owen and Katie had requested their guests make a donation to their favorite charity. Grace and David had donated to a local food bank.

"They got good weather," David said. "But then, that's not so unusual around here."

"No, it's not. But you're right. It's a beautiful day."

They held hands all the way to Arthur's Marina, where Duke and Amanda, Olivia and Eddie, and Leigh Ann and Grant were just arriving as well. The men were all in suits like David, although Duke was wearing a Hawaiian shirt with his, no tie. The women wore dresses. Leigh Ann was in a hot-pink sheath that hugged every curve, Olivia was in floral sundress with a lot of green palm fronds and some turquoise flowers, while Amanda wore a pale blue gingham sundress with a little white bolero jacket.

Grace leaned toward them. "You all look beautiful."

"So do you," Leigh Ann said. "We all look pretty good, the men included. We really should get a picture."

Amanda nodded. "We should."

Before the conversation could go any further, Duke pointed. "Company."

A boat was motoring toward them.

Grace put her hand up to shield her eyes. "Isn't that Katie's pontoon?"

Olivia looked and nodded. "It is. But that's not Katie driving it."

Leigh Ann laughed. "I should hope not."

The pontoon pulled alongside the dock. The tanned young man behind the wheel wore a short-sleeve white shirt with navy blue epaulets and white pants with a matching blue stripe down the side. Embroidered over the shirt's breast pocket was the name *Sea Dream* in three shades of blue.

The men helped secure the boat as the young

man hopped onto the dock. "Ladies and gentlemen, I am Yanni, and I am here to escort you to the Monk-Walchech wedding."

"Where is that, exactly?" Grace asked.

He just grinned. "I promise, you'll see soon enough."

David whispered in her ear. "Nice try, though."

"Thanks."

Olivia scanned the area. "What about Iris?"

Grant answered her. "She's already at the wedding location. She went with the family this morning."

They all boarded. Yanni got back behind the wheel, and off they went, leaving the island behind as they headed out toward open water. He kept the speed down so there wasn't too much spray, but Grace was itchy to see where they were going. Her guess was another private island. It made the most sense.

Although she hoped Owen hadn't bought another island, because that might mean he'd be moving. And taking Katie with him. He wouldn't do that, would he?

"You're frowning," David said. "How can you frown on a day like today?"

She turned to look at him. "What if Owen's

bought another private island and he and Katie are moving away?"

David made a face. "That's what you're worried about?"

"Well, I...yes."

He laughed softly. "Sweetheart, do you see any islands around here?"

She looked around. They'd left Compass Key behind. "No."

"Also, Owen's got a lot of money invested in his estate on Compass Key. And Katie just built that marina. And she's got all of you. I promise you, they are not moving away. I would bet you my cookbook."

She smiled. "Okay, you're probably right."

Leigh Ann, who was sitting across from them, suddenly shifted in her seat, lifting up slightly. "Oh, my. Is *that* where we're going?"

Yanni nodded, smiling. "Yes, ma'am."

They all turned to look.

Grace couldn't believe what they were headed toward. "Is that a cruise ship?"

Yanni laughed. "No, ma'am. That is the *Sea Dream*, a private yacht."

The boat, or ship, rather, was enormous. So big, in fact, that there was a helicopter parked on one of the decks and it looked small in comparison to the rest of the sleek navy blue and white vessel. Grace counted at least four more floors over the level that sat above the water. There were numerous open areas and long expanses of glass that gleamed in the sun.

As they got closer, she saw people on board. Some were staff in white uniforms like Yanni's, but a lot were in wedding clothes. She recognized Iris right away. She waved and Iris waved back.

Yanni took them to the rear of the ship, where there was a docking area at the water level. It meant they could step out of the pontoon and directly onto the ship, just as if they were docked at a marina. Another young man in a staff uniform was there to help them off.

Straight ahead of them was a wall of glass doors. The center pair were open. They went through and found a lounge were a young woman was serving flutes of champagne and two others were passing around trays of what looked like crab puffs and caviar on toast points.

Flowers and greenery were everywhere. On tall stands, draping doorways, festooning passageways. So many flowers, they perfumed the enclosed spaces.

There were more guests in the lounge, all of

them dressed for the wedding. Not too far away was an older couple with a middle-aged woman. Grace thought they were probably Owen's parents and sister.

Then another couple came into view. Grace recognized them right away from the big screen. The breath in her lungs seemed to disappear.

She grabbed David's arm, keeping her voice low. "Look. Right over there. That's Marcus and Veronica Steele." She knew they were friends of Owen's and that Katie had been to their house for dinner, but Grace had never imagined they'd be at the wedding.

He nodded. "Yes, it is. Are you going to be all right?"

She knew she was probably a little too infatuated with celebrities and other famous people, something that should have worn off after living on Compass Key for a year, but it hadn't.

And this was nothing like taking care of a celebrity at the resort. She was at an event *with* one of the most beloved couples in Hollywood. Like they were equals.

"Gracie? Look at me."

She met her husband's eyes. "I'm fine."

"You swear you're not going to go over there and ask for an autograph? Or a selfie?"

She hesitated. "Not yet."

His eyes narrowed.

"What?" she said. "By the end of the night, we'll probably be best friends. Then it won't be weird." She grinned at him. "Right?"

He shook his head like he wasn't convinced. "Try to behave yourself. We're on a ship. It's not like we can sneak out to the car and make a fast getaway."

She laughed before looking at the Steeles again. "Exactly."

Chapter Twenty-six

*K*atie blew out a breath, hoping her nerves would go with it. She smiled at her reflection in the mirrors on the closet doors because she was *very* happy, but the jitters were still with her. "Maybe I should have a glass of champagne."

From her seat on the bed, Sophie shook her head. "I don't know about that. What if it makes you loopy? You haven't had a lot to eat today."

"Because I'm too nervous to eat!" Katie sighed. "But you're probably right. I can't get married half sloshed."

Sophie stood and came over, adjusting the skirt of Katie's dress. "You'll be fine once you see him."

"You think so?"

Sophie nodded. "Plus, you'll have Uncle Hutch at your side and his arm to hold onto."

Katie was so glad for that. "And that will help."

With a big grin on her face, Sophie moved closer to her sister so they were both visible in the mirror. "Did I mention how beautiful you look?"

"Don't," Katie said. "You're going to make me cry."

"Well, you do."

"So do you." Sophie's maid of honor dress was pale pink with little crystals around the waist.

"Thanks. We should probably get your flower crown and veil on."

"Okay."

Sophie lifted the flower crown out of the florist's box as Katie crouched down a little to let her sister put it on her head. Sophie fixed the two little clips meant to hold it in place, then stepped back. "How's that feel?"

"Good." Katie straightened, then turned her head back and forth. "Secure."

"Excellent. Now comes the tricky part. The veil." But Sophie got it attached without too much trouble, thanks to the same kinds of clips. "Wow. That really does make the whole outfit, doesn't it. I mean, you looked bridal before but with the veil? Oh, Katie...."

"Don't start." Katie tilted her head back and blinked to keep the tears at bay. "I'm so ready to get to the reception part."

Sophie laughed, which instantly lightened the mood. "Don't rush it! This day is going to go by fast enough."

"I know, you're right. Again."

Sophie put the unused bobby pins away. "Can you believe you're getting married on this mega-yacht? I have to say, Owen outdid himself with this."

Katie nodded. "He did. I never imagined this was what he was planning, but it's pretty cool."

"It's definitely not the kind of thing that happens every day."

"That's for sure. I can't believe all the flowers he brought in, either. It's like a fantasy dream wedding. If that dream took place on a boat."

There was a knock on the bedroom door.

Sophie started for it. "I'll see who it is." She opened it a few inches.

"Hi. Wondering if I could get some photos?"

Sophie looked over at Katie. "It's Jahmal. He wants to do more pics."

"Sure," Katie said, and her sister let the photographer in. He'd been snapping shots all day. The videographer was set up on the fan deck, where the actual ceremony would take place.

Jahmal put her in a couple of poses, then had Sophie re-enact putting the veil on. He took more shots of them together, then asked if he could get her uncle and bring him in.

Katie nodded enthusiastically. "Yes, please."

Jahmal left, returning a few minutes later with Uncle Hutch. He was in a seersucker suit with a white shirt and a pink bowtie and his trademark straw hat. On his suit's lapel was a pink rose boutonniere.

Katie almost cried at how handsome he was. "You look so good, Uncle Hutch."

"Thank you." He held out his hands to her. "And look at you, Katie-kins. You're an absolute vision, my dear."

"Thanks, Uncle Hutch. I'm so glad you're here with me on this day."

"Wouldn't have missed it for the world."

Jahmal snapped away, his camera whirring and clicking.

Then another knock came at the door. Sophie answered it. This time it was a member of *Sea Dream*'s staff, the deck manager, a woman named Darla Green. She gave them a smile. "You look beautiful. We're five minutes out, so I'm here to escort you upstairs. We'll actually be going one level above the fan deck so you can descend the stairs, just like we practiced earlier."

"Right. This is it," Katie said. All of her friends and family were upstairs waiting. But so was the man she loved more than anyone else in the world. Owen.

Uncle Hutch stuck out his elbow, offering her his arm. "Ready to go, Katie-kins?"

She nodded. "Ready to go." She took his arm, gathered up her skirts just a little, then followed Darla.

When they reached the top of the stairs she'd be walking down, she could hear the soft hum of conversation and see the backs of everyone in the last row, if she bent down slightly. Another staff member handed Katie and Sophie their bouquets.

Christy and Dakota were at the top of the steps, too. Dakota had a basket of flower petals. When the first strains of music began to play, Christy took Dakota down the steps, then released her hand.

The little girl went down the aisle tossing petals and waving to people.

Sophie followed on Gage's arm. He was Owen's best man.

The music changed to Pachelbel's *Canon in D*. The audience stood. Uncle Hutch patted Katie's hand where it rested on his arm, and together, they started down the steps.

White and pink roses, white and pink orchids, along with lots of tropical leaves, twined around the stair railings. By the third step, she could see Owen's feet. By the sixth, his linen suit. By the eighth, his handsome, smiling face.

She smiled back.

He swallowed, the muscles in his face tensing. He took a deep breath, then blew it out and wiped at his eyes.

Everyone in the small audience was looking at them. So many happy, friendly faces. Some very new, like Owen's family. Some sort of new, like Josh and his family, and the Steeles. But most were well-known and comfortable, like her sorority sisters, and Iris.

She smiled at all of them, then put her gaze back on Owen.

Her nerves were gone by the time she and Uncle Hutch reached the officiant, who was the captain of the *Sea Dream*.

He nodded at her and her uncle. "Who gives this woman to be wed?"

Uncle Hutch lifted his chin, his smile bright, although his eyes were damp. "I do."

Then he kissed Katie's cheek, shook Owen's hand, and joined their two hands before taking his seat next to Iris.

Owen's eyes had a dreamlike quality to them. "You look beautiful," he whispered.

She squeezed his hand. His tie was pink. "You look very handsome."

As the captain led them through their vows, Katie and Owen said all the right things, but it seemed to go by in a blur and suddenly she had a diamond wedding band on her finger and Owen was kissing his bride.

And just like that, she was Mrs. Katie Monk. Happiest woman in the world.

Chapter Twenty-seven

The dancing started after dinner, a lovely meal of Wagyu filet and Florida lobster tail with fingerling potatoes, tiny green beans, and a drizzle of bearnaise sauce. Iris was full, but she wasn't about to pass up the chance to dance with Emerson.

Granted, she hadn't danced with a man in a long time. Not since Arthur. Sure, there might have been a couple of moments here or there where she'd taken a few fun steps with a guest at the lounge, or

during a guest's wedding, but she hadn't danced seriously since her late husband was alive.

Not in the way that she was dancing with Emerson. Her hand in his, the closeness, the sway of two
bodies remembering the movements of their youth
and what it was like to step into another person's
intimate space and become one with them as the
music took you away.

In his arms, she was once again transported by
the buoyancy of youthful energy. The ceremony had
already filled her with a sense of hope and peace
and that kind of promised joy that weddings and
babies seemed to bring.

They danced all the slow songs, and a few
oldies that Emerson requested from the DJ, a
young woman with pink hair and cat ears whom
Owen had flown in from Paris just for the
reception.

The song changed to something much more
upbeat. Emerson wiped the sweat from his brow.
"Why don't we get a drink?"

She nodded. "I'd love that."

They went back to their seats. Emerson pulled
her chair out for her. They'd been placed at a table
with Owen's parents, his sister, and her boyfriend.
Anita, the sister, and her boyfriend, Nate were still

dancing. Owen's parents, Lyle and Claudia Monk, were at the table.

Claudia gave them a big smile. "You two looked great out there."

"Aren't you sweet," Iris said as she sat. "I haven't danced like that in years. I'm surprised I still could!"

"You were fantastic," Emerson said. "What would you like to drink?"

"Just a club soda with lime for me," Iris answered.

"That sounds good. I think I'll have one of those myself." He looked at Owen's parents. "Can I get you folks anything?"

Lyle shook his head. "I'm good. Claudia?"

She nodded. "I'd love another glass of champagne, thank you."

"Coming up."

As Emerson headed for the bar, Claudia leaned in. "I'm guessing you two have been together quite a while."

Iris laughed. "I must admit, we have that kind of comfort level, but we only just met."

"What?" She blinked in surprise. "But you move so beautifully together. And he dotes on you like you're his sweetheart."

Iris's entire body felt like it was smiling. "What can I say? We just clicked."

Lyle sipped his drink before putting his arm around Claudia. "Sometimes, you know instantly when a thing is right." He smiled at his wife. "Don't you?"

She stared into his eyes with the most loving smile. "Yes, you do." Then she looked at Iris again. "And at our age, who has time to play games? None of us is promised tomorrow, are we."

Iris shook her head, thinking about Arthur. "No, we aren't."

Emerson returned with the drinks, holding the three glasses between his fingers like a seasoned pro. "Here you are, ladies."

"Thank you." Iris sipped her club soda, letting the bubbles join the ones that had already gone to her head from the champagne she'd had earlier. Maybe that's all this was, a champagne-induced urge, but she didn't care. Lyle and Claudia's words had sunk in.

She was not going to miss an opportunity at happiness. "Emerson?"

"Yes?"

"Let's take a little walk. I'd love to see more of this impressive vessel."

He nodded. "So would I." He was on his feet, arm extended. As she took it, he tipped his hat to the Monks. "We'll be back before the cake is cut."

They headed out through the lounge and followed the exterior walkway around the side and toward the bow of the ship. There was no land as far as her eyes could see.

Emerson had apparently noticed the same thing. "Where are we, do you suppose?"

"Probably somewhere between the Keys and Cuba," Iris said. "International waters, I'm guessing."

At the front of the yacht, they found a seating area, partially canopied by a stretch of sailcloth.

She pointed. "Mind if we sit and just enjoy the view?"

"Not at all."

As they settled in, his brow furrowed. "Why do I get the feeling we're about to have a talk?"

"Is talking such a bad thing?" And had she become that transparent?

His smile didn't reach his eyes. "It is when it goes something like, 'This has been fun but...'"

She almost laughed. "Do you think I brought you out here to let you down easy?"

"Well, didn't you?"

And to think she'd been worried about being

transparent. She took his hand. "Emerson Hutch, you are a very handsome man, a marvelous musician, as snappy a dresser as there ever was, and interesting beyond measure. But you are wretched at reading intentions."

His brows disappeared under his hat. "I am?"

"You are." She smiled at him. "I brought you out here because I am crazy about you, and I want to know what it would take to make you stay."

His mouth came open. "Y-you did?"

"Yes. I know we've only known each other for a smattering of hours, really, but unless you have the secret to turning back the clock, neither of us has time to waste."

He smiled. And then he leaned in and kissed her.

She gasped, but quickly regained her composure and kissed him back. She'd forgotten how wonderful it could be and ended up laughing, which ended the kiss. She held onto his hand. "It's been a long time since I've done that."

"For me, too. Shame, isn't it?"

"It is." She waited a moment. "You still haven't answered my question."

He frowned. "I think kissing made me forget."

"Then I'll ask again. What would it take to get

you to stay?"

"On Compass Key?"

She nodded. "On Compass Key."

He took a breath. "Not too much, I suppose. I have a little money saved up. I'm not too bad off. But I'd need a place to stay. And I can't just be sitting around. That's not who I am. I need to do something."

"How many nights a week do you play now?"

"Five nights a week. And sometimes I fill in on Sundays at a jazz brunch in the Quarter."

"Oh, a jazz brunch. That sounds marvelous." She instantly wondered why they didn't do something like that at Mother's. Maybe once a month? Might be fun. "Could you play five nights a week at the Parrot Lounge? I'll add three hundred dollars a week to whatever you're making now." Olivia might throw a fit about that but Iris didn't care.

He smiled. "Yes, ma'am, I could do that." Then his smile petered out. "But I still wouldn't have a place to live. And I can't ask Sophie to share. Young women like that need their privacy."

"I'm sure we can work out some accommodations." She didn't know how or where, exactly, but she was about to grab the brass ring and she wasn't letting anything get in the way of that. "So long as you're willing to take this leap with me and see what comes next."

His smile returned. "To be honest, the thought of going home in a couple of days had already begun to weigh on me. You're a rare sort of woman, Iris. Smart, capable, unafraid to say what you want, and as lovely as a woman could hope to be. When you paid attention to me, I felt like the sun was shining for me alone. That hasn't happened in many years."

"You're an easy man to pay attention to."

"I'm glad you think so. I never married, you know. It was my own choice. I was married to my music, I guess you could say. But music doesn't keep you warm at night the way the love of a good woman does. If you're willing to take this leap, then I want to hold your hand and jump right alongside you." He lifted her hand to his mouth and kissed her knuckles. "And if you get bored of me, or I'm not treating you like I should, you just say something and I'll smarten up, you'll see."

Something told Iris that wasn't going to be a problem, but she nodded anyway. "Same goes for me. Let's promise to be honest with each other. We've got no reason to be anything else."

"Agreed," he said.

"Then that's that," she said. "Now kiss me again."

Chapter Twenty-eight

Sophie knew Katie had been too busy to talk to Gage like she'd said she would, but Sophie wasn't upset about it. She understood. Today was Katie's day and what a day it was. Everything was beautiful. And perfect.

She glanced toward Gage, who was talking with Owen's father, Lyle. His brow was furrowed, and he looked like he was asking for advice. Probably about how to get out of his relationship with her.

Okay, everything *wasn't* perfect. Gage was still acting strangely toward her. That was the best way she could describe it. Strange. He was also a little distant. And a little distracted.

She knew the wedding stuff had to be bothering him. What else was there? At some point in the last few weeks, he'd obviously come to realize that this was not where his future lay and he either didn't know how to tell her or hadn't wanted to tell her before the wedding.

Small favors, she thought. But her heart would be just as broken in a day as it would in a week.

What did time matter? Although she supposed it was good that he hadn't done it before the wedding. It would have made things really awkward if she'd had to walk down the aisle on the arm of the man who'd just dumped her.

More awkward, anyway. As it was, he'd been stiff and quiet the whole time, acting very much like he was going through the motions. She sighed and leaned against the wall. Katie and Owen had just cut the cake and the yacht staff were passing plates out. Cake was never a bad idea. And maybe a little sugar would make her feel better.

She headed back to her table and took her seat. Jenny and Nick were there, along with Leigh Ann and Grant. She put on a happy face. No one needed to know about her troubles. "How's the cake?"

"It's worth the calories," Leigh Ann said as she cut a bite with her fork.

Jenny nodded. "I second that. I think it's vanilla raspberry almond. And the buttercream frosting is kind of amazing. Honestly, it's so good, I might have another slice."

Sophie picked up her fork as Gage approached. She quickly put a bite of cake in her mouth. It was as good an excuse as any not to talk.

He sat next to her, nodding to Grant. "Quite a

boat, huh?"

Grant laughed. "It's the most amazing thing afloat I've ever seen."

"Captain said he'll take us for a tour of the engine room if we want."

"I wouldn't pass that up," Grant said. He looked at Leigh Ann. "You wouldn't mind, would you?"

She shook her head. "Not at all. You boys enjoy yourselves."

Gage looked at Nick. "You want to join us?"

Nick nodded. "I don't know the first thing about boats, but sure, I'd love to. Thanks."

Gage gave Sophie a sideways look. "Is that all right with you?"

She wasn't sure why he was even asking. "Of course. You don't have to ask me." She almost said, "It's not like we're married," but she shut her mouth just in time.

"Well, I..." But he didn't finish whatever it was he'd meant to say.

She ate more cake and tried to figure out what it was about her that had made him realize he didn't want to spend the rest of his life with her. She'd really thought they'd had a deep connection. They had such a good time together, no matter what they were doing. Their relationship these last few months had been downright romance novel worthy. Or so she'd thought.

Clearly, she was wrong. And also lacking in something he was looking for. That understanding made the bite of cake she'd just taken tasteless. She sipped her water to wash it down.

Thankfully, the men all got up and went to see the engine room a few minutes later. Right after that, she excused herself from the table to find the ladies room, but instead she went back to the bedroom where she and Katie had gotten ready and sat in the reading chair.

She was in no mood to be around people but at least she recognized that was a terrible way to feel on her sister's wedding day. She had to shake this. At least for the next couple of hours. There was still more dancing and the tossing of the bridal bouquet and at ten, there was more food that would accompany a grand fireworks display. A buffet of small sandwiches, finger foods, and plentiful desserts was being laid out.

She put her hand on her stomach. She was still a little full from dinner. The cake hadn't helped. But what did it matter? She had fit into her maid of honor dress and now there wasn't going to be anyone to look good for.

Nice attitude, she scolded herself. Then she rolled her eyes at her own pitifulness. She really needed to snap out of it. But how could she when the breakup she was mourning hadn't even officially happened yet?

Maybe she should just confront Gage and get it over with. Just ask him straight up what was going on. Because this sort of limbo wasn't fair. Not on a day like today.

She stayed seated. It felt like a lot of work to muster that kind of confrontational energy. And she did not want to cause a scene. Not today. Not here. She couldn't do that to Katie.

Where would Sophie go if things really got bad? She was trapped on this boat with Gage until the night was over. Trapped with the man who no longer wanted her.

She sniffed, feeling worse than ever. Good heavens, she was losing it. He was just a man. The world was full of them.

Not like Gage, though. Not as strong and sweet and sexy and funny and wonderful and...a tear slipped down her cheek. She grabbed a tissue out of the bathroom and dabbed at it. She was *not* going to ruin her makeup over him.

Behind her, the bedroom door opened. She

turned to see who it was.

"Hey, there you are." Olivia grinned at her from the doorway. "Katie's about to toss her bouquet and we need all the single women. There aren't that many of us left." She laughed. "And some of us don't exactly qualify, even if we aren't married."

Sophie almost shook her head, then she stopped. Maybe that was exactly what she needed to do. Get out there and show Gage she still considered herself single. It would serve him right. Not that he'd probably care. Although if she caught the bouquet, he'd probably jump overboard. "Coming."

She followed Olivia back to the reception area and got into the midst of the other women assembled. Gage was nowhere to be seen, but she spotted Grant and Nick, so she doubted he was still in the engine room.

Whatever. It wasn't her concern. Sophie lifted her chin.

Katie held up a bouquet specifically made for the toss, a smaller, more compact version of the one she'd carried down the aisle. With the DJ pumping up the crowd, Katie turned her back to the women and held the bouquet over her head. The DJ counted as she did a windup, lifting it three times like she was about to throw.

Then, with the bouquet still in the air, she turned to face them, brought the bouquet down in front of her and walked straight to Sophie. "Here you go. This is for you. I think you're going to need it."

"What for?"

Katie's sparkling eyes and big grin made no sense to Sophie. Her sister just said, "Turn around."

Sophie turned and gaped. The other women had parted into two lines on either side of her, making room for Gage.

He stood before her, looking about as nervous as she'd ever seen him. "Sophie, I need to ask you something."

She said nothing, just nodded.

He got down on one knee.

She sucked in a ragged breath as he pulled a box from his pocket and opened it to reveal a glittering diamond solitaire.

"I've been through a lot of difficult situations in my life. Been to places I hope never to go back to. It's taught me a lot about what's worthwhile in life and what isn't. You're what matters to me, Sophie. You will always be what matters to me." He lifted the ring a little higher. "Will you marry me?"

She exhaled. And said, "Yes."

Chapter Twenty-nine

Katie welled up as Gage slipped the diamond ring on Sophie's finger. He'd been so nervous that in the last few days, he'd shut down a bit. Enough that Sophie had noticed. Katie had told him that he was making Sophie think something was wrong and he'd vowed to do better, but none of that mattered now.

If Sophie didn't understand why Gage had been acting weird, then there was no help for her. The poor man had faced many hardships during his military career, but according to him, none of them had prepared him for the arduous task of asking Sophie to marry him.

The applause from their friends and family was staggering. Katie joined in, laughing and smiling and shedding a few happy tears.

Owen came up and slipped his arm around her waist. "Well, wife, I don't think she suspected a thing."

"Oh, I think she suspected something, but it

wasn't Gage proposing." Katie laughed and looked up at him. "Husband."

He grinned. "You're stuck with me now."

"I know and it's wonderful."

He kissed her. "Did I do okay with the location?"

"You did fantastic with the location. But why didn't you tell me about it?"

He shrugged. "It started off as being a secret to keep the paparazzi away and then I just decided to make it a surprise, too."

"Well, you did what you set out to do. On both counts." There was something in his eyes. Something that made her realize he wasn't telling her something. "What is it?"

He let out a heavy sigh. "There was almost an incident, but your friends—Amanda, mainly, with some help from Duke—figured it out before it happened."

"What kind of incident?"

He explained about the paparazzi registered as guests, Duke and Amanda's part in uncovering them, and how he'd paid the boat captain to take the duplicitous pair in a completely different direction than where the *Sea Dream* was anchored.

She listened, open-mouthed, shaking her head. "Unbelievable. Those people will stop at nothing."

He stuck his hands in the pockets of his trousers. "They really won't."

"You know, we should sell a few select wedding photos to the highest bidder, then donate that money to a good charity. Or a couple of good charities. Make those wretched gossip sites do something worthwhile with their money for a change."

A slow grin spread across his face. "That's a fantastic idea." He put his arm around her again. "I definitely married up."

She smiled and leaned into him. "Somehow, we both did." She looked at the diamond band that sat next to her engagement ring. The two were so perfect together. "I love your parents, by the way. They're such nice people. Not that I expected anything less."

He hugged her close. "Thanks. I'm so glad I ended up with them."

"I am, too. I love your sister, too."

He laughed. "I understand she apologized to you for, in her words, having a fangirl freakout moment."

Katie snorted. "It was cute. And it's always nice to meet a fan. Who you are now related to by marriage."

"Listen, that does not mean you have to give her your books. She can buy them just like anyone else."

She cut her eyes at him. "I am not making your sister buy them. I will happily send them to her."

"Pushover."

She poked him in the side.

Sophie and Gage came up to them, holding hands, and both smiling.

Katie was so happy for them. "Congratulations, you two."

"Thanks," Gage said.

Sophie narrowed her eyes at her sister. "Did you know about this?"

"Not until today I didn't."

Sophie shook her head. "Do you know what I was actually thinking?"

"Yes," Katie said. "Aren't you glad you were wrong?"

Sophie smiled up at Gage. "So glad."

"All right then," Owen said. "When's the big date?"

Gage was looking at Sophie. "Soon, I think. Right?"

She nodded. "We might just do a justice of the peace thing. Or something like that. Something simple and small and just friends and family."

Owen nodded. "Sounds good."

"And there's one other thing..." Sophie started, but then looked at Gage. "Are you sure about this?"

"Yes," he said. "A hundred percent."

Sophie took a breath. "I'm moving in with Gage. Like, soon."

Katie shrugged. "Fine with me."

Sophie went on. "It's just that me living alone in Iris's house doesn't seem right. You're the one who's a part-owner. I don't have any claim to it, you know? And I realize that Iris probably wouldn't care but this way I'll be closer to you, and it'll make working easier. Cuts down on the commute."

"Yes," Owen said. "That five-minute bike ride can be a bear."

Gage grinned.

"I think it's a great idea," Katie said, almost laughing about the part her sister left out. How it would also mean Sophie would be closer to Gage.

"I'm glad you approve." Sophie's brows lifted slightly. "Would you mind telling Iris?"

Katie had a better idea. "Why don't we tell her together? I'm sure she'd like a chance to congratulate you in person."

"Okay," Sophie agreed.

Katie glanced at Owen. "Be right back."

"I already miss you," he said.

With a smile on her face, she walked with Sophie to Iris's table. Iris and Uncle Hutch were deep in conversation, but they looked up as the sisters approached.

Iris looked incredibly happy. "Congratulations are in order for both of you."

"Thanks," they said simultaneously.

Uncle Hutch stood up and kissed Sophie's cheek. "Did you know that was going to happen?"

She shook her head. "No. I actually thought he was going to break up with me."

"Well, it's a good thing he didn't," Uncle Hutch said, "I would have had to throw him overboard."

They all laughed. As Uncle Hutch sat back down, Katie put a hand on the back of Iris's chair. "We have a little news. You already know that I'm moving to Owen's."

Iris nodded. "Yes."

"Well," Katie continued. "Sophie's going to be moving in with Gage pretty soon. You're about to have your second floor back. Thank you so much for letting us live there. It's such a great spot."

Iris's eyes lit up and she looked at Uncle Hutch, grabbed his hand, gave it a squeeze, then looked back at Katie and Sophie. "Well, now. It seems *I* have some news for *you*."

"Oh?" Katie couldn't imagine what that was.

Iris nodded. "I already have a new tenant lined up."

"You do?" Katie couldn't believe that. "How? I mean, that was so fast."

"True. But sometimes things just fall in line, don't they?"

Sophie nodded, her gaze on her ring. "They do." She picked her head up suddenly. "Anyone we know?"

Iris and Uncle Hutch both laughed. Then Iris, still chuckling, said, "As a matter of fact, you do."

Katie was stumped. "Who?"

Iris's eyes gleamed brightly. "The new piano player I just hired to work in the Parrot Lounge."

Katie's heart almost stopped. Sophie grabbed her arm. "Do you mean..."

"Uncle Hutch." Katie prayed that what she thought was happening really was. "Are you staying?"

He grinned. "You bet I am."

Chapter Thirty

*A*manda wasn't surprised when, the day after Katie and Owen's wedding, the Hestons showed up at the front desk to check out early. It took every ounce of control within her not to say something to them but doing that could easily take her down a bad path. One that could reveal she and Duke had snooped in their room.

Not that she had any regrets. Her friends were her family. She would protect them to the best of her ability whenever possible.

Instead, she stayed cool and cordial as she slid Conrad's credit card back to him after clearing the few charges to the room. "We're so sorry to see you go. I hope you had a pleasant stay."

He and Julia both wore dour expressions, and neither one answered her.

Amanda held her smile. "Have a safe trip home." *And don't come back again.*

The thought made her wonder if the resort had a blacklist of guests that weren't allowed to return. If so, the Hestons ought to go on the top of it.

As the Hestons lugged their things out the door, Duke walked up. Amanda had called him earlier about a bulb out in the boutique.

She tipped her head at the doors swinging closed. "You just missed the Hestons leaving."

He laughed. "Oh, yeah? I guess the photo that Katie and Owen put up on social media last night was the final nail in their coffin."

Amanda nodded. "I'm glad they did that. It was a nice touch."

He leaned on the counter. "Maybe we should get married on a boat."

She smiled. "Maybe."

"You don't sound convinced."

"Don't get me wrong, it was easily one of the best weddings I've been to. And I've been to a lot. But I was thinking something a little smaller. A little simpler."

"Like?"

She hesitated, not sure how he'd feel about what had been on her mind. "Your parents' backyard?"

"Really?"

She nodded. "No good?"

"No, it's perfect. I love that. I never thought you'd want to do something like that."

"Because I'm fussy?"

He laughed. "You're not fussy. You like what you like. And that's just fine. But I thought you'd want, I don't know, something more formal."

"I've had formal all my life. What I want is a simple day, a nice party, and time with family and friends. And to end up married to you."

"I can get behind that."

"Good. Maybe your sister can play for us, too."

"She'd do it, no problem."

Amanda leaned in and gave him a quick kiss. "I guess we'd better talk to your folks first. Make sure it's all right with them."

"It will be. Don't worry about that."

"All the same..."

He nodded. "I'll talk to them." He jerked his thumb toward the boutique. "Guess I'd better go change that bulb. Dinner tonight?"

"I'd love to. Your place or mine?"

"I was thinking Free Willy's. For old times' sake."

The dive bar and restaurant was the first place she and Duke had gone on a real date. "Okay, that'll be fun. Six okay?"

"Perfect." He winked at her before heading toward the boutique.

She turned her attention back to her work, calling

housekeeping to let them know Bungalow 19 had been vacated early. There were no other check-outs or check-ins on the schedule today, so unless another couple decided to leave early, it would be quiet.

Carissa would be in after lunch, then Amanda would work for a few hours in the office. There wasn't too much to do. Some guest emails to catch up on; the housekeeping schedule to look over; a phone call to return.

What she most wanted to do was figure out who had tipped the Hestons off. Because that was a leak that need plugging. If it had been an employee, that person would have to be fired. It was a breach of etiquette and a breach of the employment contract that they'd signed.

She wasn't going to allow one person to jeopardize this entire place.

A little while later, after Carissa had arrived and Amanda had brought her up to speed on the day's events, most of which centered on the Hestons, Amanda finally retreated to the office.

She got all the resort business out of the way first.

Then she sent the photos she'd taken of Conrad Heston's notebook from her phone to her computer.

She wanted to be able to study them in a larger form.

As she pulled the first one up on the screen, she saw Olivia walk up to the front desk. Amanda got up from her chair and went out. "Hi."

"Hi. Do you have a minute?"

"Sure, anytime. What's up?"

"Just a little resort business. Can we talk in the office?"

Amanda nodded. "Follow me." She headed back to the office with Olivia behind her.

As soon as she was in, Olivia closed the door. The look on her face was serious. "Jenny and I have been working to come up with a list of possible employees who might have contacted the paps about the wedding."

"Really? How?"

Olivia sat across from Amanda. "Long process. Mostly by culling the names of people I felt strongly wouldn't be involved in something like that. Then I turned the names over to Jenny and she did a deep dive into their social media to see if any of them had done or said anything that might be incriminating."

"That was a lot of work."

"It was. Mostly for Jenny. But she wanted to help." Olivia smiled. "She said since you took over the wedding planning, she's felt like a weight has been lifted off of her. She wanted to help. To give back. This was her way of doing that."

"That's awfully nice. And very appreciated. Did she have any success?"

Olivia pulled a sheet of paper from her purse. "She did. But it's not a short list. There are twenty-two names on here." She slid the paper across the desk to Amanda.

"That's a lot of people. I'm not sure where we go from here other than to keep an eye on them." Amanda read through the names. Some she agreed with. Some she didn't. But if Jenny had found something online to make her believe that person might have been up to something, Amanda wasn't going to argue.

"I know," Olivia said. "And Jenny worked so hard. I didn't want to tell her that nothing might come of it."

"I don't want that to be true, either." She looked up. "We can't have someone on staff who's willing to sell out our guests. People come here for privacy. They come to get away."

"Well, everyone but the Hestons."

Amanda snorted. "Speaking of, they checked out early."

"Good."

"Yep. Only thing that's left of them now are the pictures on my camera."

"You took pictures of them?"

"No. Of the notes I found in Conrad's notebook. Not sure any of them mean anything but I have them." She pointed to her computer screen, her gaze skimming across the picture currently showing. The one with names and phone numbers. Amanda stared at the data before her as a new idea popped into her head. "Hang on."

"What?" Olivia got up and came around to stand beside Amanda so she could see the screen, too.

"What if..." Amanda trailed her finger down the screen, next to the names. "None of these names match up, but—"

"The phone numbers. Those might tell us something."

"Agreed. I can run them through the employee database, then we can do a reverse lookup on any that don't match and see what we can find out."

Olivia nodded. "Sounds good. We can divide up the work. Whatever it takes. Even if we just call them outright and see who answers."

Fifteen minutes later, Amanda hung up the phone, having just called the second to last number on her list. Then she did the same thing Jenny had done. She searched social media for the name of the person she'd just talked to. She had to be completely positive before she made an accusation. She found what she was looking for on the man's Instagram account. She looked over at Olivia. "That last number I called was for Arturo Simpson."

Olivia's brow furrowed as she looked away from her phone where she was doing her own searches. "Any relation to Raphael Simpson on the custodial team?"

"Yes. His brother. Arturo is listed as his emergency contact and they share an apartment. A week ago, Arturo, who's a warehouse worker for Winn-Dixie, posted a video of himself at a marina talking about the boat he was going to buy very soon, thanks to a big payday he had coming in."

Olivia sighed. "Raphael must have overheard us talking and figured it out. And he must have told his brother, who then decided to see what that information was worth."

Amanda nodded. "I think we need to get Raphael in here and have a talk with him."

"Agreed," Olivia said. "Do you think Raphael is in on it? That he could have been using his brother to give himself a degree of separation?"

"It's certainly possible. But it wouldn't matter. He's still guilty." Amanda wasn't looking forward to this, but it had to be done. And the sooner the better. She wasn't about to let the resort take the fall for this betrayal.

Chapter Thirty-one

*L*eigh Ann was walking back to her bungalow, her workday behind her, when her phone chimed with a distinct sound that meant she had a group text coming in. She glanced at the screen and saw it was from Amanda. Leigh Ann stopped on the path to read through it.

The message was several texts long and from both Amanda and Olivia.

Apparently, the two of them, with Jenny's help, had found the employee behind the leak to the paparazzi about Katie's wedding and after talking to him, and getting his admission to his part in it, had found him in breach of his employment agreement and fired him. A man named Raphael Simpson. He and his brother had done it together.

Jenny had added a text to say it was mostly Amanda's doing that had solved it, which Olivia had agreed with. Then Amanda had argued that Jenny and Olivia had been the ones to narrow the list down. Either way, they'd all contributed.

Leigh Ann knew exactly who Raphael was. He

cleaned the fitness center in the afternoon, and to be honest, she usually avoided him because he was a big complainer. Nothing was ever right or ever going his way. He never seemed happy. And frankly, his work usually required her to do some spot-cleaning afterwards.

She'd been meaning to say something to the group about him, but she was always so reluctant to get anyone in trouble.

Clearly, she should have made herself do it.

She stared at the screen as the incredible news sunk in. She typed out her answer. *I can't believe you all figured it out. Well done! I'm so impressed with you.*

She was, too. Having paparazzi posing as guests had felt like a dark cloud hanging over them. Like a chink in their armor. Sure, the interlopers had been caught in time, but what if they hadn't been? What if those paparazzi were there to snoop on other celebrities, like Paul? The repercussions for the resort could have been devastating.

She sent a second text, this time expressing her views on Raphael. *I know the employee in question. Very much the kind of person who thinks the world owes him something. Not surprised he was trying to hustle on the side. It's good he's gone.*

She hit Send, then tucked her phone back into

the side pocket of her leggings and continued on her way to her bungalow. She could read any replies later. Right now, she wanted to hang out with Grant and unwind.

As she followed a bend in the path, she saw Grant coming toward her from the other direction, no doubt from his studio, although he had a reusable shopping bag in one hand. She broke into a jog to meet him.

He caught her in his arms as she reached him, twirling her around once, the shopping bag swinging with her.

She laughed, her feet touching down. "I take it you're feeling better?"

"I'm a hundred percent." He took her hand as they walked toward her place.

"I'm glad to hear that. What's in the bag?"

"A few things for the dinner I'm making you."

"I can't wait. Although I hope it's healthy. I definitely overindulged at the wedding."

"Who didn't? Fun night, though."

"It sure was."

A moment of silence passed between them before she spoke again, that night very much on her mind. "You think it's okay we didn't tell anyone what happened?" That wasn't exactly bothering her, but it was sort of stuck in her mind. "It just didn't seem important, you know? Not on Katie and Owen's day."

"I agree. If I'd really had some kind of heart issue going on, that would be different. But I don't think there's any reason to alarm people over what amounted to being sore from a workout."

She grinned. "Agreed. Especially when you put it that way." They went up the steps to her place and she quickly unlocked the door. "That reminds me— Amanda and Olivia figured out which employee was behind leaking the wedding news to the paps and since he confessed, they fired him. A guy named Raphael Simpson. He was on the custodial team."

Grant's brows lifted. "How about that. Impressive work by those two."

"Jenny helped, too, though I don't know in what capacity. Anyway, I'm not happy it was a resort employee but I'm really glad it's been taken care of. We might need to send out an official statement to the staff. Something to remind everyone that that kind of behavior isn't tolerated."

He nodded. "That's a good idea." He took the shopping bag into the kitchen. "Now, you go do whatever you need to do while I get dinner ready."

She lingered. "I could help you."

He shook his head. "Nope. I've got this."

She took one step toward the stairs. "Are you sure there's nothing I can do?"

He laughed softly. "Don't you want to take a shower and change?"

Of course she did. That's what she always did when she came home. But he always let her help with dinner, too. Something was up. Or maybe, after the hospital stay, he needed to do something completely by himself? Men were strange creatures. She smiled. "Okay, fine. I'm going upstairs."

"See you in a few." He was getting a pan out of the cabinet and clearly not about to let her pitch in.

She went upstairs and took her shower, standing under the hot water and letting it wash away the day. When she was done, she towel-dried her hair before dressing in lounge pants and a T-shirt. Easy, comfortable clothing that would go perfectly with dinner and whatever movie they ended up watching.

They'd been binging a lot of classics lately. The Thin Man series, to be precise. William Powell and Myrna Loy were fun to watch on screen. A real match made in heaven. A lot like her and Grant, she thought.

She ran a comb through her still damp hair, then padded down the steps to some heavenly aromas. "That smells good."

"Thanks. You're just in time."

Her small table was set for two with a votive candle in a glass container in the center adding the flicker of firelight. And romance. He was carrying two plates over. Pan-seared salmon with a creamy dill sauce over roasted asparagus. A small glass of white wine and a tall glass of water sat at each setting.

"That looks fantastic. It's exactly what I wanted tonight. Light and healthy. Well done. And thank you."

"You're welcome." He smiled as he put the plates down. "I'm glad you approve." He held her chair for her. She sat, then he joined her and lifted his glass. "Here's to us."

"To us." She clinked her glass against his, but she still felt like something was up besides just the romantic dinner. She didn't say anything, though. Mostly to see if he did first. This was all his dinner. Might as well let him see it through.

The food was as good as it looked, maybe better, and Leigh Ann was halfway through hers before Grant said something that wasn't small talk.

"I've been thinking..."

His tone was so serious her fork froze in mid-air. "Oh?"

He nodded. "Being in the hospital does that to you. Even if it's only because you worked out too hard. It makes you take stock of your life. Makes you review your choices. Decisions you've made. That sort of thing. It's a bit of a wakeup call."

"I can see that." She just wasn't sure where he was going with it.

He met her gaze, his own as earnest and serious as she'd ever seen. "What we have is great, but..."

She put her fork down. Her heart clenched up and her appetite disappeared. She stayed quiet, letting him say whatever he needed to say.

"I love you, Leigh Ann."

"I love you, too." Her thoughts went dark. She really hoped what she was imagining wasn't happening.

He exhaled and drank the last of his wine in one long gulp. "I know your first marriage left a bad taste in your mouth. I know you're not looking to repeat that. And who could blame you? But...I want to marry you more than I've ever wanted anything in my life. And I'll do everything in my power to make our marriage the best it can be. What do you say?"

She just stared at him. That wasn't at all what she'd been expecting. Her jaw dropped half an inch as she sat there repeating his words in her head to be sure she had heard everything just right.

A few lines of worry creased his brows. "Please say you'll at least consider it."

"I will," she said.

He took a breath. "Thank you. And when you come up with your answer, whatever it is, I'll be fine with—"

"No," she said, exhaling as her entire being relaxed. She laughed, a soft, joyful sound. "I mean, I'll marry you."

Chapter Thirty-two

Olivia shook her head as she chopped tomatoes for the salad that would be part of hers and Eddie's dinner. A week had gone by, and they were *still* talking about the business with the paparazzi. Granted, nothing like that had ever happened at Mother's before. The other main topics of conversation were Jenny's wedding and how nice Katie and Owen's wedding had been. But the employee betrayal remained a top contender. "Confronting Raphael and then firing him was *hard*. Harder than just about any other work-related thing I've ever had to do before."

Eddie smiled at her from the other side of the counter. "You uncovered that embezzling scheme."

"True, but I didn't have to personally confront either of them about it. This was different. This was face to face." She blew out a breath. "It was tough. I'm really glad Amanda was there. It helped having two of us, you know?"

"I bet. I'm proud of you. The resort owes you

guys. We all do. If this place got a bad reputation..."
He frowned. "*Muy malo.*"

She nodded, sprinkling the tomatoes over the salad. "Yes, very bad, indeed."

He laughed. "Your Spanish is getting better."

"*Gracias.*" She'd been working on it these past couple of months, using an app that allowed her to do lessons at her own pace. Although focus had been a little difficult these last few days. It seemed whenever her brain wasn't occupied with work, or Eddie, it went to Simon's impending visit.

He would be here in a couple of days. And a day after that, he'd be walking Jenny down the aisle. All Olivia could do was pray that Simon had truly put the alcohol behind him, because if it seemed for one second that he might ruin Jenny's wedding, Olivia would step in. She wasn't sure yet what she would do, but she'd do *something*.

"You went awfully quiet there," Eddie said.

She smiled and picked up the cucumber to slice it. "Sorry."

"You're thinking about Simon, aren't you."

Her knife cut through the vegetable with ease, making neat round circles. "Is it that obvious?"

"It wasn't hard to guess. You want to talk about it?"

She actually did. But she didn't like to bring up the past. And she didn't want to seem angry or bitter or whatever to Eddie.

He moved around the counter to stand beside her. "Look, I get it. You're worried how you're going to feel seeing him again. You're worried that he's not really sober. That he might ruin Jenny's wedding or make a scene or do something to embarrass both of you. *Si*?"

She nodded. "Yes. All of that. And I can't help it."

"Of course you can't. The man made your life hell. Why wouldn't you be worried about all of those things? It's natural. You don't have to pretend otherwise. Especially not to me." He lifted her chin with his finger and kissed her. "Say whatever you want to say. Get it out. Don't carry all of that around with you."

She let out a little chuckle and leaned into him. "You're so good for me. And to me. I guess I just didn't want to burden you with all of it."

He spread his arms wide. "Burden me, *mamacita*. I am here for it." Then he wrapped his arms around her and held her tight. "Just like I am always here for you."

"Thank you. I am worried." He released her and she sighed. "And I don't know what to do about it."

"Talking to me is a good start. Have you talked to Jenny about it?"

She shook her head quickly. "No. We seem to be avoiding any conversations about her father on purpose. It's like she doesn't want to upset me, and I don't want to upset her. Probably means it's a conversation we should have."

One side of his mouth perked up in a lopsided smile. "You think?"

She sighed. "Okay, I'll talk to her. But seriously, what am I going to do if he does cause a scene? I cannot have that. I won't allow it. But—"

"We can handle it. Duke and me. And Grant, too. Even Gage will help, I'm sure. We won't let it happen. I'll see to it personally." He held his hands up as if to pause the thought. "If that's okay with you?"

She swallowed. "You're not going to beat him up, are you?"

He laughed. "No! I've dealt with my share of intoxicated guests on the boat. Happens more often than you think. You just have to know how to talk to them. We'll escort Simon somewhere quiet away from everyone else and get some coffee in him. We'll make sure he doesn't make a scene."

"But then who will walk Jenny down the aisle?"

Eddie tipped his head. "She has a very capable mother."

She kind of smiled. "But Jenny wants her father to do that. She invited him here for that express purpose."

"You really need to talk to her about this."

"I know. You're right. Tomorrow. First thing."

Tomorrow morning came much faster than Olivia had wanted. On her way to work the next day, she stopped at Jenny's and knocked on the door. Olivia had texted the night before to say she was going to stop by, so her visit wasn't a surprise.

Jenny answered, wearing workout gear. "Hey, Mom. Come on in."

"Off to the gym?"

She nodded. "Yeah, you know, just to see if I can do something that might make me look better by the wedding." She laughed.

Olivia smiled. "You're already the most beautiful woman on the island."

"Thank you, but you have to say that. It's part of your mom contract." Jenny went into the kitchen. "You want some coffee?"

"No, this is going to be quick. I'm on my way to the office. I wanted to have a little chat with you about your dad. I feel like we've both been sort of skirting the subject and I can't do that anymore."

Jenny's smile sunk. "Oh. Okay. What about him?"

"I have some concerns. That he won't stay sober, mostly. And that he might ruin your day in some way because of that. I can't help myself. I've had too much history with him not to think that way."

Jenny nodded. "I get that. But I promise you he's been sober for a while now. And I think I could tell if he wasn't when I talked to him."

Olivia wanted to believe her daughter, but Simon was an adept liar. And he could be very good at hiding his drinking. Until it got to the point where he couldn't. But for Jenny's sake, she just nodded and smiled and said, "Okay. That's good then."

"You don't have to be worried. You really don't."

Olivia nodded again. "Right." She hesitated, not quite ready to let it go. "And if he falls off the wagon while he's here? If something does happen? Do you have a contingency plan for that?"

Jenny didn't say anything for a minute. "No. Because nothing's going to happen."

Obviously, Jenny didn't want to talk about this anymore, but that wasn't going to solve any potential problems. "Sweetheart, I know this isn't fun to talk about. I understand that more than anyone. But you are my main concern. Protecting you and your day. Please understand that. I'm not doing this out of any malice for your father. I truly hope he's well. But if he's not, just *if*, what do you want me to do? Pretend everything's fine?"

Jenny leaned against the counter and put her hands over her face. When she took them away, she looked like she was on the verge of tears.

"Oh, sweetheart, don't cry." Olivia went to her daughter and pulled her into her arms. "I'm sure nothing will happen." She wasn't, actually. "We just need to plan for a worst-case scenario, that's all."

Jenny let out a long sigh. "I have no idea what to do if he's still drinking. Or starts back up while he's here." She looked up at her mom. "But I'm guessing you do, or you wouldn't have come to talk about it."

"I have one possible solution. Are you interested?" Olivia sensed that Jenny was struggling to deal with this reality. Simon's alcoholism had been a big part of why she and Jenny had been estranged, after all, so Olivia wanted to tread lightly.

"Yes. I'd at least like to hear what your plan is."

"It's simple. Eddie and Duke will take him somewhere quiet and get some coffee into him."

Jenny did nothing for a moment, then nodded. "Okay. That's fine. I don't think anyone will notice that too much during the reception." She looked at the time. "I should really get to the gym. I have to go see Amanda afterwards for a final check-in before tomorrow."

"Okay." Olivia knew the conversation was over. She also knew that Jenny, for whatever reason, didn't want to think about the fact that her father might end up drinking well *before* the reception. Maybe it was too much for Jenny to consider? Maybe she thought her dad could hold it together enough to still walk her down the aisle?

Olivia left with Jenny, but there was no more talk about Simon. When they parted ways before the main building, Olivia walked to her office with him still on her mind.

It was clear Jenny wasn't the only one who needed to have a talk with Amanda. If Jenny didn't want to face the possibility of what could happen, at least Olivia could make everyone around her daughter aware.

That way, if something did happen, they really would be ready to save the wedding.

Chapter Thirty-three

*a*manda's brows lifted slightly as her eyes rounded in disbelief. "You really think he's still drinking?"

"I have no clue," Olivia said. "I think I'll have a better idea when he actually arrives and I see him in person, but then again, if he is sober, that could change pretty fast. Alcohol flows pretty freely here. It's not like it would be hard for him to get his hands on some if he wanted. I'm worried this place might be too much of a temptation. Or that he'll use the wedding as an excuse to pitch himself face-first off the wagon."

Amanda nodded. There was so much fear in Olivia's gaze that she could feel it herself. "It's definitely something we need to plan for, then."

"That's all I want to do. Be ready. Just in case."

"I appreciate the heads up. I knew about your past with him, obviously, but I didn't realize it might still be a problem."

"And maybe it isn't. Maybe I'm completely

wrong." Olivia splayed her hands. "I'd love to be wrong about this. I really would. But if I'm not…"

"Right. I get it." She leaned in, putting her forearms on her desk. "How are you feeling about seeing him again?"

"I'm not exactly looking forward to it. But I won't have to see him much. And I think it's good that Jenny spends a little time with him now that she knows the truth about what really happened between her father and me all those years ago."

Amanda hoped there wasn't going to be any turmoil, but weddings seemed to pull everyone's emotions to the surface. "As the wedding planner, it's pretty easy for me to come up with an excuse to stop by to see Jenny. That is, if you want me to check in and see how things are going after he gets here."

"I'm sure it'll be fine," Olivia said. "But I'll keep that in mind. Have you ever had to deal with a situation like this before?"

"I've had to intervene with a few inebriated guests that were on the verge of being a problem. But never a father of the bride so intoxicated that he was the issue. Do you have a plan if he decides to drink?"

"Eddie. And Duke." Olivia sat back. "I've talked to Eddie about this, and he said he'd handle it and that he'd get Duke to help. Possibly Grant and Gage, if need be. But the plan is just to get Simon away from the ceremony to somewhere he can be sobered up."

"Does Jenny know about that?"

"Yes. I talked to her. Although she seems to think if it happens, it's going to happen at the reception."

"And you think it could happen before?"

"I do." Olivia knotted her fingers together. "Am I overreacting? I mean, nothing's happened yet. And it might not. Am I dwelling on my past too much? Being overprotective? You're a mother. What would you do in my situation?"

Amanda smiled. "Exactly what you're doing. You're not overreacting. Your fear that Simon could ruin things is founded in his past behavior. Until you see what he's like now, you have nothing else to judge him on. Because I'm sure he's gotten sober before."

Olivia rolled her eyes. "More times than I can count. It's never stuck." She looked away. "I wish he was more like Grace. She just decided to quit and did it."

"I don't think her problem had been going on for quite as long as Simon's. And she had a lot at stake. You're the expert on him, but it seems to me he'd been drinking a long time. I got the sense with Grace that it was just something that had become an issue the last year or so."

"True." Olivia gathered up her purse. "I've taken up enough of your time. I know we both have work to do. Eddie is going to speak to Duke, but if you want to talk to him, too, that would be great."

"Listen, I'll not only talk to him, I'll make sure the staff knows not to offer Simon a drink. And to keep an eye out for him, to make sure he's not indulging via other means. We'll get through this. I promise. You just try not to worry about it too much, okay?"

Olivia smiled. "Okay. Thanks."

As soon as Olivia left, Amanda texted Duke. *You around?*

I can be. Ten minutes?

Perfect. She went back to work until he arrived, which was much faster than ten minutes. She smiled as he came in.

"You rang?" He shut the door.

"I did. Thanks for coming so fast. Has Eddie reached out to you?"

"About the potential Simon situation?" Duke nodded as he took a seat. "He has."

"And you're good with helping?"

"Completely. I was hoping we could use the conference room in this building as a possible place to bring him. Considering that the wedding is going to be right out there on the beach and the reception will be in the Treasure Pavilion."

"That would be fine. You have a key, right?"

"I do. I don't know what's in there now but I'm going to make sure there's at least a couch and a couple of chairs. I can get coffee from the restaurant."

"Sounds good. I guess there's not much else we can do until then."

"Well...maybe."

She picked her head up. "Meaning?"

"Meaning if we can tell he's not sober when he gets here, then we talk to him. Or someone does. Try to get proactive."

"You mean Olivia? I don't think that will work. Not with their history."

"I don't either. I meant maybe Eddie and me. And Nick. Having your future son-in-law tell you to sober up for the wedding might be just the kick in the backside Simon needs. Especially since Nick's a doctor."

"Hmm." Amanda thought about that. "Not something I'd considered, but it could work. If Simon cares enough to travel here, then he ought to care enough to be sober on the big day."

"In theory, I agree with you. But I don't think it works that way with alcoholics."

"I'm sure you're right."

Duke shifted in his seat. "You want me to talk to Nick?"

Amanda shook her head. "No, I'll do it." She stood. "In fact, I'll go right now."

"I'll walk with you." He got up. "I'm headed back that way anyway."

They didn't hold hands as they walked. As much as Amanda might have liked to, she shied away from public displays of affection when they were both on duty, as it were. Although she did give Duke a quick kiss before they separated. "See you tonight."

He nodded. "You know it."

She watched him head off to his next job, then went inside the medical office. She rang the bell at the desk, which had no receptionist, since there had never been a need.

Nick came out. "Hi."

"Hi. Do you have a second?"

"For the wedding planner?" He grinned. "I have whatever time you need. Unless someone comes in with a bleeding headwound, of course."

"Of course." She laughed. "This will be quick. As I'm sure you know, Jenny's dad has a history of alcoholism. Olivia is concerned, with good reason, that he might drink while here and cause an issue."

Nick frowned. "That wouldn't be good."

"No, it wouldn't be. We do have a plan, however. If we have reason to think he is drinking again when he arrives, then you, Duke, and Eddie, will have a man-to-man conversation with him and make him understand he needs to be sober for the entire wedding. Ceremony and reception."

Nick leaned against the front desk. "You think that will work?"

"I hope so. If he drinks before the ceremony or at the reception, to the point that he's on the verge of being a problem, then Eddie and Duke are going to take him to a private room and sober him up. But I'd like not to get to that point."

"Me, too."

"So you're willing to speak to him if the need arises?"

Nick straightened. "Without question. I'll do whatever you need me to do to make this day perfect for Jenny."

Amanda nodded. "That's all I needed to hear."

Chapter Thirty-four

A trill of excitement and a quiver of nerves coursed through Jenny. The pontoon carrying her father toward Compass Key was in sight. It had been a while since she'd seen him, and truthfully, although she hadn't really wanted to talk about it with her mom, she was concerned he might have lapsed.

If he was drinking again, it would crush her, because he'd promised he was done with all of that. Beyond her disappointment, she wasn't sure how she'd handle it. Maybe let her mom step in? She supposed that wasn't exactly the most adult thing to do, but Jenny didn't want his visit to turn into some big fight between herself and her father. Not when he was supposed to walk her down the aisle.

The possibility of a fight worried her. A lot. She and Nick had already had to send Yolanda to the mainland. Would they have to send her father home? Because she wouldn't allow him to be part of her wedding if he wasn't sober.

Some lines weren't meant to be crossed.

"Almost here."

Jenny turned to see her mom walking toward the dock. She nodded. "Almost. Thanks for coming."

Olivia touched her daughter's hand. "Whatever you need. I'm here."

"Thanks."

Olivia shrugged. "Doesn't hurt that Eddie's driving the boat."

Jenny laughed, grateful for the moment of light-heartedness to break the tense mood she was in.

As the pontoon came alongside the dock, Jenny went to meet the vessel, aware that her mom had stayed behind.

Her dad stepped out from under the pontoon's canvas cover. "Hi, Jenny."

"Hi, Dad." He looked older than she remembered. Thin, except for a rounded belly that hung over his belt a bit. His hair was gray and sparse, combed over the top of his head in a failing attempt to hide a bald spot. His nose and cheeks were flushed with a ruddiness she didn't recall, either. And it didn't look like the side-effect of too much sun.

Her heart sank. Time had not been kind to her father, but he hadn't been kind to himself. She smiled all the same. The way he looked had nothing to do with her love for him. "I'm so glad you came."

He smiled back. "Wouldn't miss my baby girl getting married for anything. Can't wait to meet this young man of yours. A doctor! How about that? I hope he knows he's marrying up."

"Dad." Amused, Jenny shook her head.

Eddie got the boat tied off and secure.

Simon climbed out onto the dock and gave her a hug. She hugged him back, hoping with all her heart that the whiff of something she smelled was just aftershave.

As he let her go, he glanced toward Olivia. Behind him, Eddie brought his suitcase off the boat. Simon tipped his head toward Olivia. "Who's your friend?"

Jenny looked back, realized he was talking about her mother, and shot him a look. "Dad. That's Mom."

His jaw went south an inch. "That's your mother?"

Jenny took her in with new eyes. She *had* changed a lot this last year. Lost weight. Gotten a new hairstyle and blond highlights. Started wearing more makeup and getting facials and her eyebrows done. Plus, she had a golden glow year-round from all the time she spent outside and probably a little bit from her relationship with Eddie. She looked younger and prettier than she had when she lived in Ohio, that was for sure.

No wonder Simon didn't recognize her. "That's her."

He tugged at the track suit jacket he wore. "She's changed, huh?"

Jenny shrugged, not exactly sure if he meant that as a good thing or a bad thing. "She takes good care of herself, that's for sure. Come on. We'll say hi and then I'll take you to my place."

He grabbed the handle of his suitcase and nodded. She couldn't read the expression on his face, but her guess was that he didn't know what to make of Olivia's transformation.

Jenny was proud of what her mother had accomplished. Deciding to take care of yourself was a big deal. Putting that plan into action took work and dedication and perseverance.

They walked toward her. Jenny stopped a few feet away. "Hey, Mom. We're going back to my place."

Olivia nodded. "Nice of you to come, Simon."

"Thanks." He rubbed at his chin. "You, uh, you look good."

"Thank you." Olivia didn't return the compliment, but Jenny understood. To say the same thing back to him would have been a lie. "I guess I'll see you around."

Simon nodded, but hesitated, not quite ready to go. "You really own part of this place?"

"I do," Olivia said. "One fifth of the island and the resort. And I'm the CFO."

Jenny smiled. She was so proud of her mom she had to chime in. "She uncovered a major embezzling scheme last year. The previous accountant and the head chef were in on it together. She recovered almost ten million dollars of the resort's money."

Simon's brows went up and he whistled. "Pretty impressive. If I had known you were that good with money, I might have kept you around."

Jenny watched as her mother's gaze went steely and her mouth firmed into a hard, indignant line. She wasn't about to let her father start things. She took hold of his arm and leaned in. "Dad, Mom left you. Let's not pretend it was the other way around."

He mumbled something she couldn't quite make out and started walking. She went with him and glanced back at her mom.

Her mother was smiling. She mouthed the words, *thank you*, and gave Jenny a little wave.

Jenny smiled, too, returning the wave, then

shifted her attention back to her dad. "How was your trip?"

"Fine, just fine." He was looking around, taking it all in. "Quite a place."

"It sure is."

They chatted the whole way, catching up. She watched him closely. His gaze lingered on the pool-side bar and his eyes followed a server who went past with a tray of drinks. But neither of those things meant he was drinking again. She understood staying sober had to be a struggle.

When they got closer to the house, she decided to ask him flat out. "How's the sobriety going?"

He laughed. "Don't you worry about me. I'm just fine."

And that, Jenny thought, was not an answer. "Just curious how many days you have now. Isn't that how they count it? In days? You get a coin or a chip, right?"

He laughed again. "I don't need any of that nonsense. I'm doing great."

None of that reassured her. She stopped at the bottom of the steps, wanting to see the conversation through before they went upstairs. "I thought you were going to meetings. You told me you were."

"I was, but the meeting place changed and it's a

little far for me now. Especially since I changed jobs and my new one is in the opposite direction. I promise, when I get back, I will find another place closer. But you're what's important to me now." He looked up at the house. "Is this where you live?"

"Yes. On the top floor." She was well aware that he'd changed the subject. She didn't like that he'd stopped going to meetings. That felt like a warning flag.

But maybe she was reading too much into it. Or maybe she wasn't. She started up the steps, only to realize her father was struggling with his suitcase. She grabbed the handle and took it from him. "I've got it."

At the top of the stairs, Nick opened the door and came down to meet them, taking the suitcase from Jenny. He stuck his hand out. "Hey, I'm Nick. You must be Simon. Nice to meet you, sir."

"You, too, son."

Nick hauled the suitcase up and into the house, leaving the door open for Jenny and her dad.

She waited for him to enter, then shut the door behind him. "I hope you don't mind but we have you in the office on an air mattress, but it's a good one. I promise. As comfortable as a regular bed."

He smiled. "I'm sure it'll be fine."

"I hope so. Nick's mom is in the guest room. Or will be. He's going to pick her up soon." She looked at Nick for confirmation.

He gave her a nod. "I'm actually just on my way to get her now."

Simon put a hand on the kitchen counter. "I can't wait to meet her. Although I might take a little nap, if that's all right. All that travel wore me out."

"Sure," Jenny said. "The bed is made up and you should have everything you need. I'll show you."

Nick glanced at her. "You need me for anything, just text."

"I will," Jenny said.

"Back in a bit."

Simon lifted his hand. "Good to meet you. I look forward to chatting later."

"Same here, Mr. Rhodes."

"Please, Simon."

Nick nodded. "Simon."

Jenny took her dad into the office, rolling his suitcase behind her. "Do you need anything? Something to drink? A snack? I'm making baked ziti with sausage for dinner tonight. We're not doing a rehearsal dinner, since it's such a small wedding, and we walked through the ceremony with the officiant last week."

"Sounds good to me. I'm fine. A little nap and I'll be ready to go."

"Okay. One more thing. About Nick's mom...she can be a handful. I don't know what she'll be like around you, but she can be sort of critical. Anyway, I just wanted to give you a heads up."

"I appreciate that." He leaned in and kissed her cheek. "It's so good to see you. You seem very happy."

"I am. Really happy." She smiled. "I'm glad you're here. Have a good nap."

"Thanks." He shut the door as she stepped out.

She stood in the small hallway for a moment, staring at the closed door, and trying hard to shake the feeling that things weren't as they seemed with her father.

She'd never wanted to be wrong so badly in her life.

$\mathcal{M}$ arried life was pretty awesome. Katie pulled her hair into a messy bun, then changed into leggings and a sweatshirt along with sneakers. Owen was waiting for her on the boat. They were going out for a ride and to have lunch.

Because of Jenny and Nick getting married so soon after Katie and Owen, she and Owen had decided to postpone their honeymoon until a little later. That would also allow her to be here for when Uncle Hutch returned from New Orleans.

The honeymoon plan right now was to head to Owen's ranch in Montana during the summer for a couple of weeks. Generally, the resort was a little slower then because that was the hottest time of the year. Wasn't always true, but usually. And the guests who did come didn't do much more than spend their time in the pool or out in the ocean water.

Until Montana, Katie and Owen were trying to do a few little daytrips where they left work behind and just spent time together. Today was one of those days.

Rika had packed them a cooler with all kinds of good things to take along with them. Katie went down to the kitchen to pick it up.

"Good morning, Mrs. Monk," Rika said with a smile.

It would be a while before being called Mrs. would sound commonplace. Katie grinned. "Good morning to you."

Rika added a few more things to the cooler, then closed and secured the lid. "You're all set."

"Thank you so much."

"You're welcome. Enjoy your day."

"I'm sure we will." Katie stopped at the couch to kiss Fabio's fuzzy head. He was sprawled in a puddle of sunlight and felt like he was on fire, which was something he enjoyed immensely. Hisstopher was upstairs on the deck that had a cat door leading out to it. So far, he and Fabio were getting along pretty well. They weren't exactly best friends, but there was no fussing at each other either, so all good.

From the house, she went straight down to the dock. Owen was on his red speedboat. Gage was on the dock, talking to him.

"Morning, boys." She handed the cooler over to Owen.

He took it, giving her a big smile. "Morning, wifey."

Gage cleared his throat. "That's my cue to go. Have fun."

Katie took Owen's hand into the boat. "Yeah, you, too." She knew for a fact that he and Sophie were going to the mainland later to see a movie and have lunch.

Owen held onto her hand and used it to pull her into an embrace. "You look fetching today."

"I still love you even when you lie."

He feigned a look of hurt. "I didn't lie. You do look fetching."

She laughed. "Okay, if you say so. Where are we headed today?"

"I thought we'd go out to Kissing Key. It's actually two small islands that are connected by a sandbar at low tide. Hence the whole kissing thing." He pulled away from the dock and got them moving.

"Fun." She dug her sunglasses out of her bag and sat back. "I'm in for whatever."

"Good, because first I need to stop by First Light Charters on the mainland. That'll be the only work part of the trip, I promise."

"Oh? What's there?"

"That's who I chartered the *Sea Dream* through. They gave me a discount with the stipulation that I take a photo with the owner outside the business to display."

"I'm surprised you agreed to that."

"I know. Not my usual way of doing things, but..."

"But what?"

He grinned. "I want to buy that yacht. And I'm trying to talk him into selling it to me."

"Owen. Really?" She had no idea he'd liked it that much.

He nodded. "Why? Did you not like it? I just thought it would be such a great way to get away and see the world without all the hassle of conventional travel. Plus, we made a pretty big memory there."

"Well, that's very sweet. But you have your own plane. It's not like you have to wait at the gate as it is now."

"I know, but there's something romantic about traveling by boat. Don't you think?"

She nodded. "I can see it. But piloting a boat like that would be so much work."

He laughed. "I wouldn't do it. We'd hire a crew. Captain, first mate, a cook, cleaners, the whole nine yards. Then you and I and Gage and Sophie could just lounge around in the sun and enjoy ourselves. When we weren't working, of course."

The idea was starting to grow on her. "It does sound kind of fun. I might feel a little bad being away from the resort for too long, though."

"Most of what you do for the resort can be done remotely, and we'd have internet via satellite, so it wouldn't be a problem."

She leaned back, stretching her arms along the sides of the bench seat. "How many does the *Sea Dream* sleep?"

"Fifteen crew members and up to twenty-two guests or passengers."

"Wow. I should have paid more attention when I was on it. I didn't realize."

He nodded. "Did you see the master bedroom? It's beautiful."

"I didn't, actually. We were in one of the guest suites to get ready, but it was really nice. Bigger than I would have thought, and the bathroom was every bit as nice as yours."

He smiled. "Ours."

"You know what I mean." Adjusting the way she thought about his house was going to take some time.

"About that. The house, I mean. If there's anything you want to change or redecorate, go for it. I know it's a bit of a bachelor pad. I recognize that. So please, put your touch on it. If you want to paint or change the floors or anything, I don't care. I mean, I'd love to know what you're thinking about doing so I don't get shocked by pink fake fur or a wall of sequins, but I'm open to change."

"Pink fake fur?" She laughed. "Where would that go exactly? Next to the wall of sequins?"

He lifted one shoulder. "Probably. In your office."

"I don't really have an office." That was one downside to moving into Owen's. She didn't have a dedicated office.

"You will. The guest room at the opposite end from where my office is? We need to turn that into your workspace. I know you need an office. You work more than I do some days."

"Yeah?" She bit her lip. "You wouldn't mind?"

"Not at all. I want you to have your own space." He chuckled. "I don't need your readers coming after me because your book production drops off."

She got up to stand next to him. "They probably would."

"Oh, I'm very aware of how rabid they are. Anita

told me at the wedding that I am not to interfere with your writing schedule."

"Did she really?"

"Yes." He glanced over at her. "I told you my sister was a huge fan."

She put her arms around him. "So...I'm not sure about the pink fake fur, but that wall of sequins sounds interesting."

She imagined him rolling his eyes behind his dark sunglasses as he shook his head. "Have I created a monster?"

She shook her head. "I won't do anything that crazy. But I do like the idea of creating my office from scratch."

"Good, because there's a decorator coming in next week to help you."

"You spoil me."

He slipped his arm around her, keeping one hand on the wheel. "And we've only just begun."

Chapter Thirty-six

The wedding menu food list was the top sheet of paper clipped to Grace's clipboard. She ran through it with David while he took inventory. Since the wedding was tomorrow, he had one last morning shipment of product coming in to make sure he had everything he needed.

Jenny might be Olivia's daughter, but Grace felt just as protective as if she were her own. Even if she hadn't felt that way, she wouldn't want Olivia to be disappointed. Or Amanda, who'd pitched in to help organize. Grace wasn't about to let anything go wrong for her friends, at least not where the reception was concerned. That was all she could really control.

But the reception was a big deal. It was the married couple's first meal as husband and wife. It was them coming together with family and friends. And it was a chance to impress their guests with the spread.

She and David stood in the big walk-in fridge. He hadn't bothered to put a jacket on, but she had.

It was *chilly* in here, but men were generally tougher about things like that. Not to mention, David was in a chef's coat. She called off the items on her list, then ticked them off or made an ordering note as he responded. They were almost done.

She read the next item. "Shrimp."

He counted the bags of individually frozen jumbo shrimp on the shelf. The starter was a tropical shrimp cocktail. "Need. But not frozen. I want to get fresh. Put a note to call Fernando."

He was the local shrimp guy. She marked that on the sheet. "Next is filets."

"Have." He tapped the cryo-vacced whole filets that he'd be portioning out later. "These are reserved for the wedding."

She nodded and added a checkmark. "That's all of it. Now I need to go see Chantelle and make sure she's good, too."

She and David walked out of the giant refrigerator. He made sure the door was closed. "What else do you have to do?"

She gave him the inventory sheet, then looked at the paper that had been underneath it. Her to-do list. "Make sure the bartender has his supplies and we're set. All he's doing is beer, rum punch, and champagne. There will be water, iced tea, and coffee, too."

"Seems like there's not too much left for you to do, then."

"Nope. Why? You need help?"

He smiled. "I could always use a little help. Feel like turning out ten pounds of carrots? Or dicing twenty pounds of mangos?"

She laughed. She was much better with the front of the house than the back, but if he genuinely needed her... "Not really, but I can. Although my knife skills aren't—"

His laughter cut her off and he shook his head. "I'm teasing. I've got the line crew on it. We're in good shape. But I love how willing you are."

She exhaled in relief. "I'm so glad to hear that."

He gave her a quick kiss. "I'll be home as soon as I can tonight. Early, if possible, since tomorrow is a big day. I was thinking maybe we could sit in the hot tub. We haven't done that in a while. Maybe I'll even bring pizza home. What do you think?"

"Pizza? In the hot tub?" She looked at him like he was crazy to think she'd argue that. "I'm in. See you tonight."

"Tonight." He winked at her before going back to work.

She walked next door to Chantelle's pastry area. The young woman was sitting on a stool in front of her worktable, piping bag in hand, creating buttercream roses on a flower nail, a metal device that sort of looked like a giant thumb tack.

Behind her, one of her assistants was making batter for something else.

Grace watched Chantelle work for a moment. With the flat tip on her piping bag, she exerted just the right amount of pressure and formed petals on the nail until a beautiful rose appeared. "Those are gorgeous, Chantelle."

"Thanks." Chantelle used her lifter to scissor the rose free, then place it down on a sheet tray with all the others she'd made. Once they dried, they'd be put on the cake. Or so Grace assumed.

"Just checking in to see that you have everything you need and how things are going."

"Good. I'm almost done. The only thing I need is the real flowers. Once those arrive, I'll need to work with them for a bit, but I won't be putting the real stuff on the cake until tomorrow right before service."

"I'm so glad you made the cake happen. Amanda told me there was a little blip in the ordering."

Chantelle smiled as she started another rose.

"There was. As in they forgot to do the actual ordering. But it's not like I was going to let them get married without a cake. Besides, they weren't after anything too elaborate. Three tiers with cascading flowers." She finished the rose, added it to the tray, then looked up again. "You want to see it?"

Grace nodded enthusiastically. "I would love to. Wedding cakes are just so much fun to look at."

Chantelle hopped down off the stool. "Come on, I'll show you."

Grace followed her to the pastry walk-in. "What flavors did they go with?"

"According to the notes that Amanda had, they wanted tropical. So the bottom layer is our famous key lime cake with raspberry buttercream, the second layer is coconut cake with pineapple jam, and the top layer is passionfruit with white chocolate ganache."

Grace's mouth was watering. "That all sounds amazing."

"They're all really good. And I'm not just saying that because I made them." Chantelle opened the walk-in and turned on the light. There, in the center on a stainless-steel cart, was the cake. Three perfect rounds in pristine white banded with a ribbon of aqua. From the top tier, which was elevated by four columns, a bouquet of flowers spilled down the side and over the other two tiers.

"Chantelle, you are so talented. It's perfect. And absolutely beautiful, but it looks done. You're really going to add more flowers to that?"

Chantelle nodded. "I am. You'll see. It's going to look even better. There will be a big bunch at the top, then I'll intersperse the real ones with the sugar flowers."

"I can't wait to see it. And taste it. Great job."

"Thanks." Chantelle came out and closed the door.

"I still don't think there's any way you're going to fit all those icing roses on there."

"You're right. I'm not. I'm doing five dozen passionfruit and white chocolate ganache cupcakes that will be boxed up as take-home favors for the guests."

"You are? I had no idea. I didn't even know we had boxes for that." For their favors, Katie and Owen had given everyone a Montblanc pen with the wedding date engraved on it.

"We don't. I got them from my parents' bakery and Amanda okayed the extra funds to cover them. But it had to be done. Amanda mentioned the other day that there were no favors and that it was too late to order anything, so I suggested that."

"You're a gem, you know that? Wow, way to go above and beyond."

Chantelle grinned. "I don't mind. I'd want someone to do the same thing for me someday."

"Speaking of, how are things with you and Jamarcus?"

Chantelle let out a quiet laugh. "They're going all right. He's very nice."

"So are you," Grace said. "And if he doesn't treat you right, he's in trouble."

"He's treating me very well." She picked up the flower nail again. "He brought me a heart-shaped pizza for dinner the other night."

Grace put her hand to her heart. "Oh, the early days of love are just the best. I'm very happy for both of you."

"Were you and Chef like that?"

With a smile on her face, Grace nodded. "We were. He once made me a heart-shaped steak."

Chantelle laughed. "I like that." Her smile went a little shy. "And I like Jamarcus very much. He's really sweet. And it helps that we both work and live here, you know? Makes things a lot easier."

"I'm sure it does. I'm happy for you both. Love is

so much fun." Grace knew from experience how hard relationships could be, but things between her and David were so good now that they'd gotten through the rough patch caused by her drinking. "See you later."

Chantelle went back to her roses. "Later."

As Grace left, her phone went off with an incoming call. It was Amanda. Grace answered. "Hi."

"Hi. I figured it would be easier to tell you what's going on with a call than a text, so I hope you don't mind."

"Not at all. Wedding business?"

"Sort of," Amanda said. "Olivia thinks Simon might use the wedding as an excuse to overindulge, which could be disastrous. I was hoping we could tip off the staff that will be serving at the reception, especially the bartender, so they know not to serve him."

"I can handle that, but won't he complain if he asks for a drink and doesn't get one?"

"Maybe. But he's also supposed to be sober, so doing that would be a pretty big sign that he's quit the program. I don't think he'll want that getting back to Jenny."

"Then we need to be sure he's not sneaking alcohol, either."

"My thoughts exactly."

Grace nodded, understanding all too well what a mess Simon could make of things. "I'll be sure the staff knows."

"Thanks," Amanda said.

"Anything else I can do to help, just let me know." Grace would be watching him. More than most people, she knew what to look for. Might as well put that experience to use.

Chapter Thirty-seven

*I*ris had never been so pleased to get a surprise phone call than the one she'd had that morning. Emerson was arriving a day earlier than expected. Now she stood on the dock, eagerly waiting for him. He'd been away for nearly a week and a half. Far too long. Thankfully, Nico had gone to pick him and his things up.

As the pontoon came alongside the dock, Iris wasn't surprised to see the number of suitcases the man had. He was a natty dresser, and clothes took up space.

Didn't matter, he'd have the whole second floor to himself now that Sophie had moved in with Gage and Katie was settling in at Owen's.

Behind her, several porters with low, flat rolling carts arrived.

Nico tied the boat off and Emerson stepped out, greeting her with a smile and a kiss. He had a leather satchel over one shoulder. "Hello, my darling Iris. I feel like I've been away from you for a year."

"I feel the same way. I'm so glad you came back early."

"Wasn't hard to do. With all the traveling I've done over the years, I'm pretty good at packing. I had some help from friends, too."

"When is your container arriving?" She knew he had more than just the suitcases on board.

"In a couple of weeks. Thankfully, I was able to pack the essentials. Amazing the amount of mementos you accumulate over a lifespan, eh?" He shook his head. "I tried to pare them down but perhaps I'm too sentimental. It was awfully hard."

"No need," she said. "You'll have room with the girls moved out. And I was thinking that we could do a little showcase on you in the marquee area of the lounge. You know, there's that shadowbox that really isn't being used other than to house the name of the lounge, which is already over the door, and the drinks menu, which can be read just as easily inside."

"You're spoiling me." He smiled. "Whatever you think is best."

"Well, that's what I think is best. We need to let our guests know just who you are. I want to talk to the girls about selling your CDs in the boutique, too. We've had great success selling the cookbook by our head chef. I can't see why it would be any different for our new musical talent."

He put a hand to his heart. "I don't know what to say. Other than thank you."

"You're welcome." The porter she'd called had the luggage cart loaded. She gave him a nod. "Thank you, Kenny. Those go to the second floor of my house. You know the way, no need to wait."

The porter took off and she and Emerson followed at a slower pace, her arm through his.

Emerson let out a happy sigh. "Part of me doesn't believe I've done this. It feels like a dream. Who gets a new opportunity like this so late in life?"

She smiled. "It's never too late to try a new path, is it?"

He looked at her and smiled. "Never."

"Do Katie and Sophie know you're back early?"

"No. I didn't want to bother them just yet. Tomorrow will be plenty of time. I know them. They'd want to drop their own plans to help me move in and unpack and I don't want them to feel obliged to do all that. I can handle it."

"Well, I hope you don't mind but I've already enlisted Vera's help for you today. I imagine it'll mostly be hanging things up?"

He nodded. "A lot of that, yes. In one of my bags

is carefully wrapped awards and such from over the years."

"Oh, those sound perfect for displaying. Would you mind? I'm sure they're very dear to you, but I love the idea of showcasing a few of those."

"I wouldn't mind at all."

"Marvelous."

As they reached the house, Kenny was just taking the last bags up. Vera stood on the second-floor porch, smiling down at them. "Hello there, Emerson."

He waved up at her. "Nice to see you again, Vera."

"You, too. Are you here to stay?"

He nodded. "I am."

Happiness suffused Iris. Together they went up to the first floor. Vera came down the inside steps to meet them.

"I hope you're hungry," Vera said. "Lunch is just about ready."

He set his satchel down near the couch. "Smells good, whatever it is."

"Crustless quiche with sausage, sun-dried toma-toes, a little onion, and about four different kinds of cheese. There's salad, too."

He smiled. "You two sure do eat well. Sounds

fantastic. I should probably go check things out upstairs first."

"I'll go with you," Iris said, looking around for her four-legged crew, but the cats must all be out and about. Not a single one showed their face. Well, the food would bring them back. She headed for the steps. "I can show you around. Officially."

"All right." He followed her up. "Nice that there are inside and outside steps."

She nodded. "It is. But as you can see, we put doors in to keep things more private. Also, I have three cats and they'd be in your business if not for these doors."

He laughed. "I wouldn't mind. I think I would have had a cat myself if not for all the traveling I did. Always did like Katie's Fabio."

"They're good company," Iris said. She gestured toward the main living area, which encompassed the kitchen, dining room, and family room all in one big space. "I know you stayed here for the wedding, but as you can see, most of the furnishings are still here, since I provided them. If you need any of this out to make room for your own things—"

"No, no. It's wonderful as-is. Bigger than my place in New Orleans, so I wouldn't have anything to fill it with." He took a few steps toward the sliding doors. "Never had a view like that, either. Boy, that water is something. All that blue. Inspires a person."

"I'm sorry there's not a piano up here."

He turned to see her again. "Oh, I don't mind that. I have my keyboard. And I promise it won't bother you. I have a pair of headphones that I connect so I'll be the only one to hear it."

She smiled. "I don't think your playing would bother me one iota."

"It might, depending on when I was playing." He laughed. "I keep late hours. Part of the business. Although I suppose those will change a bit now. How late is the Parrot Lounge open?"

"I believe until two a.m. but no one expects you to play that late."

He shrugged. "I played until four some nights in the Quarter. Wouldn't bother me. But we can work all of that out."

She indicated behind her. "Bedrooms and the office are back here."

Once she'd showed him the rest of the place, they went back downstairs. Vera was taking the quiche out of the oven and, sure enough, three desperate furry faces meowed silently at her through the sliding glass doors.

Iris chuckled as she went over to let them in. "Emerson, meet Calico Jack, Anne Bonny, and Mary Read, all named for the pirates that made Compass Key their safe haven once upon a time."

"Is that right? Real pirates?" He came over to the cats, crouching down to scratch their heads. "What a handsome bunch you are. I'm your new neighbor, I hope we can be friends."

Calico Jack pushed against Emerson's leg while Mary Read closed her eyes under Emerson's pats.

Iris looked on. "I think you're already friends. I'll give you a packet of treats to take upstairs with you in case they show up on your porch. They do like to travel."

"Well, they're welcome anytime."

Vera brought plates to the table. "Not on my table they're not." She shooed Calico Jack, whose little nose was sniffing the quiche-scented air pretty hard. "Don't even think about it, pretty boy."

Iris went onto the porch, got the treat bag from the side table, and give it a shake. That brought the three cats outside. She tossed some treats around for them, then went back in. "That should keep them busy for a little while."

They all sat down to eat.

Emerson wasn't shy about his appreciation for

the food. "This is outstanding, Vera. Do you cook like this all time?"

She smiled. "I cook most of the meals, so yes, I guess. I enjoy it. Do you cook?"

He laughed. "Afraid not. But there's so much good food to be had in New Orleans that eating out seemed like the thing to do. Gumbo, jambalaya, fried chicken, crawfish etouffee, fried catfish, po boys, oyster stew—"

"You're making me hungry while I'm eating," Iris said.

Vera's eyes narrowed. "You know, that's one region of cooking I've never really delved into all that much, but I'm thinking it might be time to see what it has to offer. Iris can't eat too much heavy stuff, but I bet I could come up with some ways to make it healthier. And still taste good."

Emerson forked up another bite of the quiche. "I bet you could. And I'm willing to give you my opinion on anything you make."

Iris and Vera both laughed. Iris reached over and squeezed Emerson's arm. "You are welcome in this house anytime."

He smiled at her. "Thank you for making me feel so at home."

She smiled back. Life was taking on a brand-new shape for her and she'd never felt more blessed.

Chapter Thirty-eight

*L*eigh Ann strolled hand in hand with Grant on the beach, the sand soft and cool underfoot, the sound of the gentle waves the perfect backdrop to the evening's activity. "We really should do more of this."

He nodded lazily. "I agree. Why don't we?"

"Because...I have no idea. We forget we can? We get caught up with other stuff? We're too tired?"

"Probably all of those. But no more excuses. We need to get out here. To be in this." He stopped, pulled her in close, and stretched his arm toward the water. "Look at that. The way the moon reflects. The way the stars gleam. It's better than anything I could ever put on canvas. It's inspiring."

She leaned against him. "It really is. We're blessed to have this as our backyard. One of them, anyway." She hesitated a moment but there was no better time to talk about what was on her mind. "About that. Where are we going to live after we get married?"

He turned his head, kissed her, then answered. "I don't see any reason to change the way things are now. I say we keep both houses and split our time as we see fit. I know it's much easier and makes more sense for you to be here on the island. I don't want to make your life harder. So why not use the bungalow as our main residence and use the mainland house as a retreat. If that's okay with you?"

She nodded. "It's perfect, actually. I just wasn't sure you'd want to do that. Although I don't know why. You're about the easiest man to get along with that's ever walked the face of the Earth."

He laughed. "I don't know if I'd go that far. But I see no point in fixing something that isn't broken."

She held him tighter. "I love you."

"I love you, too, my beautiful muse." He kissed her again. "Have you told anyone we're engaged yet?"

She shook her head. "No. I didn't want to steal any of the spotlight from Jenny and Nick. There will be plenty of time for us after they've had their day."

"You're a remarkable woman, you know that?"

She shrugged. "I'm just me."

"And that's what makes you so remarkable."

They started walking again, hand in hand, no

real destination before them. There were other guests out walking, all of them seemingly in their own bubble of happiness. It was a perfect evening.

When they reached the section of beach adjacent to the main building, they turned and went back along the beach to where they'd started, taking their time.

Even so, they shortly neared the path that would take them into the heart of the island and back to her bungalow. Grant stopped again in front of the last pair of chaise lounges. "Let's just sit for a few minutes. What do you say? Soak up a little more of this amazing night."

"I say these chaises belong to that last bungalow but as long as the guests staying there aren't using them, I'm in."

"Tell you what," he said. "We'll just use one. How's that?" He pulled her down onto the chaise with him, making her laugh.

"You've convinced me."

They stretched out together and just enjoyed the evening. She sighed. "I could stay like this forever."

"Me, too."

A few moments later, a couple came stumbling out from the path onto the beach. They staggered toward the water, giggling and laughing, and finally plopped down a few feet from the reach of the waves. He had a small bottle of some kind of liquor. He took a drink from it, then passed it to the woman. In the darkness, it was hard to tell what kind of alcohol it was, but that wasn't an important detail.

Leigh Ann sat up but kept her voice down. "That's not good. Those two are clearly intoxicated. And way too close to the water."

Grant nodded. "Do you want me to do something?"

"No. I'm going to call security. It's part of what they do. They'll escort them back to their room. It's easier for them to be the bad guys, if that's the role someone has to play. The guests aren't going to argue with them as much. You know what I mean?"

"I do."

She pulled her phone out and sent a quick text to the security staff on duty, alerting them to the issue and the couple's location as well as where she was.

About five minutes later, two of the staff showed up, the word Security visible in yellow on the backs of their dark polo shirts. The largest of them, Russell, Leigh Ann knew pretty well. He did the overnight shift, but generally got a workout in at the fitness center before he went home in the morning.

Russell gave her a nod as he approached the couple, who were still drinking. "Evening, folks. You look like you're having a good time."

"We are," the man slurred. "A ghreat time."

"Glad to hear that. Unfortunately, we don't allow glass containers on the beach, so I'm going to need that bottle. I'd be happy to carry it back to your bungalow for you. Which one are you in?"

The woman turned and Leigh Ann suddenly realized who she was, her blond hair gleaming in the dim moonlight.

"I'll have you know my son *lives* here," Yolanda said, "He's the island's doctor. Dr. Nick."

Leigh Ann didn't know who the man was with her. Most likely a guest she'd hooked up with. Which was problematic on its own.

"Where are you staying then, ma'am?" Russell asked.

"In his house. Now you just run along and leave us be."

Leigh Ann shook her head. "This isn't good."

"Nope," Grant said. "Not one little bit."

With a hand on Yolanda's shoulder, the drunk

man got to his feet. "Where's the bar? We'll go there."

"Sir, it might be better if you called it a night." Russell held out his hand. "And I'm still going to need that bottle."

The man yanked it out of reach. "My daughter is about to marry her son. And her mother owns this place."

"Uh-oh," Leigh Ann said.

"You can say that again." Grant groaned softly. "Hello, Simon."

"Should we call Olivia? Or Jenny? No, forget that. Jenny can't see this the night before her wedding."

"I concur." He nudged Leigh Ann. "Video this. Just in case. But I'm going to help Russell. See if I can defuse this situation and get them to agree to go home. If I can, Russell and I can walk them back and then I'll explain everything to Nick and Jenny when we get there."

"Okay. I'll follow until the house, then just meet you back at the bungalow." She pulled up the video camera on her phone and watched the screen as Grant approached them.

"Hi, Yolanda." He stuck his hand out. "I'm Grant. I'm a friend of Nick's and one of the ushers at the wedding tomorrow. You must be Simon, Jenny's dad?"

Simon looked slightly stunned, either from the alcohol in his system or that someone knew who he was. Maybe a combination of the two. At last he took Grant's hand and shook it. "Thath's right."

"I'm really looking forward to the wedding. I'm sure you are, too."

Simon nodded, going a little maudlin. He sniffled. "I am. Thath's my little girl."

Grant waited a beat. "Are you going to be all right to walk her down the aisle? Maybe you should call it a night, huh? I'm sure Yolanda would agree that getting your beauty sleep is important." While he was talking, he eased the bottle away from Simon and tucked it into his back pocket.

Leigh Ann smiled. Bless Grant. He was such a good guy.

Russell extended his arm. "I'd be happy to escort you back, Miss Yolanda."

Russell was a handsome, fit man. Leigh Ann didn't think Yolanda would be able to resist. It only took a couple of seconds for Leigh Ann to be proven right.

"Well," Yolanda said, taking Russell's arm and

smiling up at him. "I guess we should be getting back."

Simon heaved out a sigh. "Yeah, all right."

Grant shot Leigh Ann a look, giving her a quick nod. She smiled at him, even though she knew whatever happened next was probably not going to be fun.

Chapter Thirty-nine

*O*livia sat on the porch with Jenny and Nick. She didn't want to say that Yolanda and Simon had been gone an awful long time, but they had. The beach on Compass Key was a finite stretch of land. There were only so many minutes one could spend walking it.

She'd thought it was a bad idea from the get-go when Simon had said he and Yolanda were going out to walk so they could get to know one another better. They had hit it off surprisingly well at dinner, something Olivia hadn't anticipated.

In retrospect, she supposed they were very much alike. They were the kind of people who expected a lot from the world in exchange for doing as little as they could. And they were both over-indulgers in a lot of ways. Was that being too harsh on Simon? She wasn't sure. She really didn't know what he'd been up to these past however many years. She only knew what he'd been like when they'd been married.

And it was the rare leopard that changed its spots.

"Nick?" Jenny said quietly. "Maybe you should text your mom. See if everything's all right. I suppose they could have gotten lost."

He stood up, phone in hand. "I will, but I have a better idea. I'm going to look for them. There's no telling what my mother's got your father roped into."

Jenny frowned. "Or vice-versa."

A knock on the door turned all their heads toward the front of the house. Olivia had a bad feeling about this. She jumped up. "I'll get it."

She went straight to the door and pulled it open. Grant and Russell, one of the resort's security guards, stood there with Yolanda and Simon between them. The pair was glassy-eyed and wobbly.

The smell of alcohol was unmistakable.

Olivia's heart sank, her worst suspicions realized. Her jaw tightened but she kept her mouth shut. There would be time for recriminations later. She moved out of the way. "Grant, Russell. Thank you for...bringing them home."

She didn't know what had happened for Simon and Yolanda to end up needing an escort, and she wasn't sure she wanted to.

Russell gave her a nod. "You folks have a good night."

"You, too." She looked at Grant and ignored Simon and Yolanda as they filed past. She kept her voice down. "Is everything okay?"

He looked over her shoulder. "They were clearly inebriated and drinking on the beach." He reached into his back pocket and produced a mostly empty fifth of bourbon. "I took this off Simon. Would you mind if I talked to Nick?"

"No, come on in."

She turned to walk in with him.

"Dad?" Jenny was standing in front of her father, blocking his way as he tried to go into the office where the air mattress was. "What's going on?"

Simon put a hand out to the wall steady himself. "Jus' having a little fun, sweetheart. Thath's all."

"This is fun? You think this is *fun*? The night before my *wedding*." Her hands were clenched, and she looked on the verge of an angry cry. "You told me you were sober. You promised me."

"An' I will be in the morning. Don' you worry about it."

Her jaw was a tight line of fury. "You're right. I'm not going to worry about it. Because you're not walking me down the aisle. In fact, I don't want you at the ceremony at all."

With that, she stormed off to the bedroom. The

slam of a door followed shortly. Simon looked after her with a confused expression.

Olivia didn't think he grasped what had just happened.

Nick sighed and stared at his mother. "What part did you have in all of this?"

She shrugged innocently. "No one told me he wasn't supposed to drink."

"I actually did, Mom." Disgust curled Nick's lip. "I think Jenny's got the right idea. Neither of you belong at the wedding."

"No, Nick. Please," Yolanda pleaded. "I didn't know about Simon's drinking. I really didn't. He had the bottle with him!"

"I believe that, but I don't believe you didn't know." His expression softened slightly into one of pure disappointment as he looked at Simon. "As for you, you had to know that Jenny would be devastated if you drank. All your promises of sobriety... What was the plan? Did you really think she wouldn't figure it out?"

Simon shuffled awkwardly. "I...I didn't..." He started to cry.

Olivia cleared her throat softly. "Nick, make some coffee for both of them. I'll go talk to Jenny. Simon, go sit on the couch. Yolanda, you, too."

Yolanda snorted. "You're not the boss of me."

"*Mom*," Nick said. "Sit."

Yolanda sat. Olivia went to the bedroom and knocked softly on the door. "Jenny? It's me, Mom. Are you okay?"

"No," came the grumpy, tearful response through the door.

"Can I come in?"

A brief pause. Then, "Yes."

Olivia opened the door. Jenny was sitting on the edge of the bed, staring at the floor. Olivia went to her and wrapped her in a hug. "I'm sorry."

"You were right. I should have listened to you. Once a liar, always a liar. I should have known."

"It's in a child's makeup to want to believe in their parents. If it were any other way, the world wouldn't function. You're not to blame. He is."

Jenny sniffed and leaned into Olivia, arms around her mother's waist. "He's ruined everything."

"No, he hasn't. He's just ruined his own chance to be part of your special day. Nothing he's done changes how much Nick loves you or how beautiful tomorrow is going to be or how proud I will be to watch the two of you join your lives."

Jenny sighed. "Thanks. I'm glad you're here."

Olivia kissed the top of her daughter's head. "I'm

glad I am, too." She hesitated, knowing Jenny was in a fragile state. "Can I ask you for one favor?"

"What?" Jenny looked up.

Olivia sat beside her. "Don't make a decision about letting your dad walk you down the aisle right now. Wait until the morning. See how you feel then. I know he's lied to you and let you down, but you only have one father."

Jenny's brows knit together. "You're the *last* person I expected to say something like that."

Olivia smiled tentatively. "There was a time I thought I'd never get to attend your wedding. It was a feeling that haunted me. I cannot imagine what it would have done to me if that had happened. So I can understand what your father is feeling right now."

Jenny went back to staring at the floor. She let out a big sigh and put her hands on her knees. "He's not going to change. So why should he be rewarded?"

"You're right. He shouldn't be. Not for what he's done. But I don't want you to have regrets about this either. Someday, when you look back on this, I want you to have the memory of walking down the aisle with your dad. Because there won't be a second chance for that to happen. Just something to think about. That's all." She smoothed a few strands of hair back from Jenny's face.

"Okay. I'll think about it. But that's all. No promises."

"That's all I'm asking. Thank you." She exhaled. That had gone better than she'd expected. "Would you prefer it if I made your father sleep at my place tonight?"

"I can't ask you to do that."

"You don't have to. I'm offering. And there is no alcohol in my house, so he won't be able to sneak any."

"You'd do that?" Jenny laughed. "I know you would." She nodded. "I think that would be best. If he stays here, I'm going to worry about him getting into our stash all night. Or going back out with Yolanda. Or on his own." She threw her arms around Olivia. "Thanks, Mom. I really couldn't do this without you."

"I'm happy to help. I wish things had gone differently."

"Me, too. But I guess I needed to see this for myself." Jenny's frustration showed on her face. "I just wanted to believe him so much that I couldn't see any other possibility. I'm sorry."

"No need to apologize. Get some sleep. Big day tomorrow."

"Yeah, that's for sure. Night."

Olivia got up and headed for the door. "Night."

Yolanda and Nick were on the porch, talking softly. Her head was down, and she looked miserable. Olivia hoped for her sake that Nick allowed her to attend the wedding, too. She stuck her head out. "Sorry to interrupt. I'm going home and I'm taking Simon with me."

"Okay," Nick said. "Thanks."

Olivia gave him a nod, then walked over to the couch. Simon was hunched over, elbows on his knees, face in his hands. "Get your pajamas and your toothbrush. You're spending the night at my place."

Chapter Forty

*a*manda directed Mindy and her delivery team to bring their boxes of flowers into the staging room. Later on, the room would become the backup plan for Eddie and Duke, in case they needed to put Simon somewhere.

She didn't think that was going to be a problem, however. Not after the long email Olivia had sent out telling them all what had transpired at Nick and Jenny's last night. That poor child. And poor Olivia. What a mess.

To think she'd had to let Simon sleep at her place. That couldn't have been fun. Not with their history. But Amanda knew that Olivia was a very different woman than the one she'd been back then. There was no way Simon would get away with anything. Or be allowed to bully or intimidate Olivia. Not now. Not these days.

It was, however, still up in the air as to whether Simon would be walking Jenny down the aisle. As far as Amanda knew, he might not even be attending the wedding. Despite everything she knew about the man, a small part of her heart ached at that possibility. But she'd stand by Jenny, no matter what she decided.

Her wedding. Her day. Her decision.

She stood nearby as the florist, Mindy, from Key Largo Florist, opened the boxes. Amanda leaned in to inspect them, but with Mindy on the job, there wasn't much need. "These look great, Mindy. Another fantastic job."

Mindy smiled. "You're welcome. This one is special, I know."

"It is, you're right."

Mindy hefted one box that was still closed. "These go to Chantelle. She's probably not in yet, though, is she?"

Amanda checked the time. "No. She's not due for another hour. I can take those over to her workstation for you."

"Yeah? That would be great, thanks. I'm going to get my guys working on the beach site, so we're ready for the ceremony."

"Great. The chairs should be set up by now. I know resort staff is working on the pavilion, too." A small group of resort staff was helping set up for Jenny and Nick's wedding, but they were being paid out of the wedding budget, not from the resort's accounts.

It wouldn't have bothered Amanda if the resort had paid for it. Nick and Jenny were basically employees themselves, Nick as the resort's doctor, and Jenny by handling some of the PR, but Nick had insisted.

As Mindy left with her crew, Olivia came in. "There you are. I figured you'd be around here somewhere. How's it going?"

"Everything is on schedule. Maybe even a little bit ahead. We're in great shape. How are things with you?"

Olivia sighed and rubbed her chin. "Simon was up half the night. Part of the time he was crying, the other part he was pacing the living room talking about all the ways he could make things right with Jenny."

Amanda grimaced. "Sounds like you didn't get much sleep."

"I could have used more but what was I going to do?" Olivia shrugged. "He might not be my husband anymore but he's still Jenny's dad."

"Right."

"And of course, he's still sleeping." As if to emphasize her tiredness, Olivia yawned. "Sorry."

"No worries. Have you heard from Nick? I'm wondering if Yolanda's going to be there. Do you know?"

"I haven't a clue."

"Speaking of clues, any idea what Jenny's going to decide?"

Olivia shook her head. "I'm on my way over there after this. I just wanted to come by and snap a few pics of the progress to show her. I thought that might help lighten her mood, if that needs doing."

"Good thinking. Get the bridal bouquet. That's sure to put a smile on her face."

"Oh, definitely. Where is it?"

"Right here." Amanda opened the box to reveal the gorgeous spray of white and aqua roses, greenery, and gold ribbon.

Olivia sucked in a breath. "That is *so* pretty. Mindy does a great job, doesn't she?"

Amanda nodded. "She does."

Olivia snapped a couple of photos.

Amanda couldn't help but ask. "Are you for or against Simon being in the wedding?"

Olivia's mouth bunched to one side. "I don't really know. And it doesn't matter. It's Jenny's decision."

"You must feel one way or the other."

"I do." She shook her head. "It's hard. I'm mad at him. Maybe more than Jenny, because I think what she feels is betrayed. The realization that her father not only lied to her previously, but has continued to lie to her, that had to be very hard."

"I'm sure it was."

"If he apologizes to her in a sincere enough manner, I think she should let him participate. I even went to bat for him last night, asking her to wait until this morning to make her decision. But if she doesn't want him there, I'll stand by that, too."

"This is so difficult."

"It is."

Impulsively, Amanda hugged her friend. "Anything you need, either of you, just say the word."

Olivia sniffed. "Thank you but don't go making me weepy now. I'll never make it through the rest of the day."

"Sorry." Amanda smiled. "Whatever happens, it's going to be a beautiful ceremony."

"Yes, it is. Now I'd better go. I'll text you when I know something."

"Okay." Amanda watched her leave. She hoped that everything could be resolved, and that Duke and Eddie wouldn't even have to think about keeping an eye on Simon.

But Amanda wasn't a Pollyanna. She knew better than to think one evening had changed anything. For Jenny's sake, she prayed the day was as easy as it should be. And that she was left with happy memories instead of a black mark that she'd look back on for the rest of her life.

The only thing Amanda could do toward that goal was what she was already doing. Making sure things ran smoothly and on schedule so that all Jenny had to worry about was coming down that aisle and saying her vows.

Granted, Jenny had some thinking to do about who would be accompanying her down that aisle, but after that, everything should be smooth sailing.

To that end, Amanda went outside and straight down the path that Jenny would be walking later that day. She needed to see for herself how things looked on the beach.

She was not disappointed. She'd organized numerous weddings at the resort now and her wedding staff, a group of resort employees who knew exactly how things were supposed to go for such events, were doing their usual excellent job.

Rows of pretty gold bamboo folding chairs were set up in shallow, half-moon rows with an aisle down the center. At the end, a beautiful new gold bamboo arch, bigger and better than the previous one the resort had owned, awaited them. Mindy and her team were draping everything with swathes of white and aqua tulle, thick lengths of satin ribbon, and festooning it all with fresh flowers and greenery.

Amanda felt a sense of peace settle over her as she surveyed the scene. The sky, water, and sand were a flawless backdrop. Everything was going to be as perfect as it could be for the ceremony.

From there, she went to the Treasure Pavilion and checked on how that was coming. Tables draped in white were set up around the dance floor. In front of all of it was the head table, where Nick and Jenny would sit together as husband and wife for the first time.

Amanda looked up. The beams of the pavilion had been wrapped in fairy lights so that as the sun set, a warm glow would light the festivities.

Soon Mindy's crew would be over here, adding more of the same touches that they were doing beachside.

The food and cake weren't even in question. David and Chantelle were consummate professionals. They'd deliver nothing less than the best. It was just what they did.

For that, Amanda was grateful. They allowed her

to put on the kind of weddings that every bride dreamed about.

Nick and Jenny's would be no different. So long as his mother and her father didn't become the elements that turned it all into a nightmare.

Chapter Forty-one

*K*atie rapped on the door three times. She laughed, looking at her sister. "It's weird to knock on what used to be our door."

"I know," Sophie said.

Uncle Hutch opened it, greeting them with a big smile. He was in his bathrobe, not what Katie had expected, as he'd invited them for breakfast. "My two favorite nieces!"

Sophie chuckled. "We're your only nieces."

He wiggled his head as he moved out of the way to let them in. "Still my favorites."

"And still nice to hear," Katie said. "Morning, Uncle Hutch. Did we show up too early?"

"Not at all. I'm just running late."

"No worries." That wasn't like him at all but he had just traveled. He got a pass for sleeping in. She hugged him. "I can't believe you got in yesterday and didn't tell us until last night. It was such a surprise to get your text."

"I am a rascal, aren't I?" He hugged Sophie, too. "I just didn't want you girls rushing over here to fuss with all of my nonsense. I know you have lives to lead. Husbands and fiancés to take care of. And I'm very capable of taking care of myself."

Sophie grinned. "Even so, you should have at least texted when you arrived."

He put his hand on his heart. "I solemnly swear that the next time I move into your neighborhood, you will be the first to hear of my arrival."

Katie snorted. "Good to know. How was your first night on the island?"

Before he could answer, Iris, dressed in only a bathrobe, came out from the bedroom. "Did I hear voices? Oh!" She giggled as she stopped short. "Good morning, girls."

Katie's mouth fell open. She looked from Iris to her uncle then back to Iris. "Did you spend the— You know what? Never mind. I don't want to know. You're both consenting adults and that's your business."

Sophie was still staring, her mouth also ajar.

Uncle Hutch went up on his tiptoes. "Sophie-doll, you'll catch flies that way."

Sophie closed her mouth. She glanced over at Katie. "This is like one of your books."

Iris tightened her robe around her as she went into the kitchen. "Not exactly, Sophie. Your sister's books don't generally have heroes and heroines with gray hair and Medicare plans." She got the coffee down, a red metal canister with the Community label on it. A New Orleans staple that Katie instantly recognized.

"Maybe they should," Katie said.

"Maybe," Iris agreed. "Coffee, girls?"

"Heck, yes." Sophie grinned. "We did come for breakfast. Or did you forget, Uncle Hutch?"

"No, no. I remembered. I just, uh, lost track of time." He cut his eyes at Iris. "It's very easy to get distracted here."

Katie couldn't hold back a laugh. "Hey, I meant it about the consenting adults. Whatever you two want to do is up to you." She held her hands up. "I don't need an explanation. I don't need to know anything."

"Same," Sophie said. "Is there something we can help with breakfast-wise? You know, while you two put clothes on?"

Uncle Hutch laughed. "That would be marvelous. Vera was kind enough to stock my fridge with bacon, eggs, butter, cheese, and all sorts of delicious ingredients." He gestured toward the kitchen. "Go forth and cook."

Katie rolled her eyes good-naturedly. "I see now why we were invited over."

"Right?" Sophie said.

"Well, at least I made the coffee." Iris lifted her chin, her cheeks a little pink, and headed back to the bedroom.

Uncle Hutch followed her.

As soon as the bedroom door closed, Katie looked at Sophie and they both started giggling. And whispering.

"Can you believe those two?" Sophie said.

"I guess I can. And hey, good for them." Katie opened the fridge and took out the eggs and bacon.

"I agree," Sophie said. "Love has no age. And shouldn't. I think it's great. It's just a little shocking. But not in a bad way."

"Yep." Katie looked in the fridge again. "How about a veggie scramble? There's a green pepper in here and there are onions and tomatoes on the counter. If you work on that, I'll get the bacon started."

Sophie pulled a knife from the cutting block. "I'm on it."

Together, they fried a package of bacon, stirred up the veggie scramble, which got topped with a sprinkling of sharp cheddar, and made a few slices of toast.

When Uncle Hutch and Iris came out, dressed,

they put their efforts into setting the table. Before long, they were all sitting down and taking their first bites.

Uncle Hutch raised his cup of coffee. "Thank you, girls. You did a wonderful job. I feel spoiled."

Katie noticed he was looking at Iris when he said the last part. "I hope you always feel that way, Uncle Hutch. And I want to say that I'm so glad you're here but also that I'm really happy for you and Iris. I truly am. It makes my heart glad to see two people I love finding such a connection."

Iris smiled. "Thank you, Katie. That was very sweet."

Sophie nodded. "Ditto to what she said. Love seems to be in the air lately around here. First Katie's wedding, then my engagement, and you two, and now today's wedding. Must be something in the water."

"Then pour me a glass," Uncle Hutch said. "I think love is grand. It was very kind of Jenny to invite me to her wedding on such short notice." He winked at Iris. "Although I think you had something to do with that."

"I might have," Iris confirmed. "But she couldn't very well deny me a plus one, now could she?"

Katie took half a piece of toast and buttered it. "Iris, no one can deny you anything."

Her smile was demure, but her eyes were twinkling. "I suppose that's a little true."

Katie gestured at her uncle with the slice of toast. "You need to know that about her, Uncle Hutch. No one says no to her."

Sophie nodded. "Iris is a woman who gets things done. Sometimes before you realize they even need to *be* done."

Iris waved a hand through the air. "You girls. You make me sound like some kind of superhero. I have merely lived long enough to learn effective motivational techniques."

Uncle Hutch looked amused. "Nothing wrong with any of that." He grinned at Iris. "Power is sexy. Especially on a woman." He quickly changed the subject. "My first official night playing at the Parrot is in two days. I expect you both to be there."

"Wouldn't miss it," Sophie said.

"We'll bring Owen and Gage, too," Katie added. "Make a night of it."

"That reminds me," Iris said. "I want to turn the front marquee—you know, the big glass shadowbox?—I want to do a whole thing about Emerson in there. Some of his awards, a nice headshot, a little written history. Something so our guests know what kind of talent we've got. And since you, Katie, are the writer and in charge of communications, and Emerson *is* your uncle, I thought you could head that up and get it done."

"Sure," Katie said. "I'd love to."

"Good." Iris ate a bite of eggs. "I want to sell his CDs in the boutique, too. I guess you'd need to talk to Amanda and Olivia about that. Either way, will you take that on as well?"

Katie loved how much Iris wanted to put Uncle Hutch front and center. "Absolutely. I'll get on it first thing tomorrow. I think it's a great idea. Especially if we can offer some signed ones. Look how well the cookbook is doing."

Iris nodded. "That's exactly what I was thinking. Thank you for spearheading that."

Katie smirked, shifting her attention to her uncle. "See? Exactly what I was talking about. Before you know it, you'll be an international superstar."

He laughed. "Well, that sounds marvelous, but all I'm really worried about is keeping my new employer happy."

Iris smiled and reached out to touch his hand. "You don't have to worry about that, trust me. I am."

Chapter Forty-two

*J*enny had stayed mad at her father until she'd seen him at her front door. He'd come to apologize. That part, she'd expected. She knew that while the apology was sincere, there was every chance he'd break all the promises he was making.

She shook her head. "Dad, I know you mean all this now. Just like I know you're sober now, because you were at mom's last night and couldn't drink. But I also know that at the first possible opportunity, you're going to drink again."

"No, Jenny, I swear. I'm done."

"You've said that before. Why is it different this time?"

"Because it is. Because I see now how selfish I've been. To do this to you right before your wedding... It showed me just how bad things have gotten."

She hadn't planned on letting him walk her down the aisle, but her heart was softened by the fact that it was her wedding day. She decided to use her power for good in that moment. "I'll tell you what—you can walk me down the aisle so long as you stay sober. I expect you to stay that way, too, even through the reception. If you drink, I'll have you removed."

He'd started nodding instantly. "Of course, anything you want. I totally understand."

"Listen to me. I'm not done. If you drink again and I find out about it, if you don't get back into meetings as soon as you get home, if you don't regularly attend those meetings, then you and I are done. No phone calls, no email, no texts, nothing. I will not have that kind of toxic behavior around. Not when Nick and I intend to start a family. So not only won't you see me, but you won't be a part of your future grandchildren's lives, either."

He stared at her, eyes welling. He nodded. "I understand. It's hard, Jenny."

"Dad, life is hard. But there are tools to make it easier. And if you want something bad enough, it can be done. You'll make it happen. No excuses. You've had a lifetime to get yourself together, haven't you?"

He nodded sheepishly. "Yeah."

"I don't know why I wasn't enough of a reason for you when I was little, so maybe I won't be enough of a reason for you now, but those are my terms. Think them over. If you agree, show up at the wedding, dressed to walk me down the aisle. If you don't agree, or you don't think you can do it, pack your stuff and leave, because we're through." Harsh words, she knew, but she felt like she had no other recourse.

"O-okay. But I don't need to think about it. I agree."

She shook her head. "No, you do need to think. You need to let everything I've said sink in. Now, I have to get ready. I hope I see you later, but if I don't, I'll understand what your decision was."

After a moment, he nodded. "Bye, Jenny." He turned and went down the steps.

She closed the door and let out a breath. Nick had gone to Duke's to get ready and Yolanda was in the guest room, occupied with her own preparations.

Olivia would be over soon to help Jenny get dressed. She'd promised that Eddie would be around to keep an eye on Simon.

Jenny frowned. A grown man shouldn't need keeping an eye on, but she was thankful that Eddie was willing all the same.

But the ball was in her father's court. She wasn't

going to think about it anymore. If he didn't show up, she'd walk the aisle with her mom.

Jenny took her shower ,and about a half hour later, Olivia was at the door to help her get into her dress. Leigh Ann was there, too. She'd offered a while back to help with hair and makeup and Jenny had happily agreed.

Both of them were dressed and ready to go, both of them beautiful. Olivia's dress was a dusty blue with a little beadwork that sparkled every time the light touched it. Leigh Ann's dress was a floral-patterned sheath, nipped in at the waist.

Getting ready didn't take that long. The makeup they'd practiced was simple. Her hair was being left long with a braid at each temple pulled back. Leigh Ann added a few soft curls with a big barrel curling iron. Olivia attached the veil, securing it with the flowered combs.

She stepped back and clasped her hands together in front of her chin. "Oh, Jenny. You look beautiful."

Jenny stood and turned to see herself in the full-length mirror. She took a deep breath, smiled, and nodded at the two women. "Thank you both so much. I couldn't have done this without you, Mom.

Leigh Ann, I love the hair and makeup. They're perfect. I am so grateful to both of you."

Leigh Ann got her phone out. "Stand together. I'll take a pic of you."

Olivia moved next to Jenny. Jenny took her mom's hand. Both women had been taking photos since they'd arrived, which Jenny was happy about. She'd wanted this moment just for them. The hired photographer would start taking pictures right before she went down the aisle.

When Leigh Ann finished, Olivia adjusted one side of Jenny's veil. "Almost time to go."

Phones vibrated. Leigh Ann held hers up. "That's Amanda. They're ready."

Olivia and Jenny walked together, Leigh Ann behind them. Guests stopped to watch Jenny, smiling and taking pictures and offering their congratulations. She felt like a movie star. But her heart was in her throat, waiting to see what her father's decision was.

They went into the main building. Amanda was waiting for them in the lobby. She smiled as they joined her. The photographer, Rob, husband of Mindy the florist, was there. He started snapping away.

Amanda took Jenny's hands for a second. "You look stunning, Jenny. Nick is one lucky guy, but having seen him a few minutes ago, I can promise you that you're a pretty lucky woman."

Jenny laughed. "I know. I can't wait to see him."

Leigh Ann excused herself to take a seat. Jenny looked around.

There was no sign of her father. She did her best to act like she was okay with that. She made herself smile. "Mom, I think you're going to have to—"

"She's right. You're the most beautiful bride."

Jenny turned to see her dad, cleaned up, shaved, in his suit, coming toward her. He looked nice. "Dad."

He nodded. "I'm here. I was just getting my boutonniere on."

She held it together. "I'm so glad."

"I should go," Olivia said softly.

Simon shook his head. "I don't mean to impose, but I think it would be nice if you walked with us." He looked at his daughter. "What do you say, Jenny? Would it be all right if your mom walked with you on the other side? She is the reason we're here, after all."

Jenny nodded. "Yes." That was all she could

manage at the moment, or she'd break down. It was an incredibly kind gesture on her father's part.

As her parents stood on either side of her, Mindy came out and handed Jenny her bouquet. Rob took more pictures. Then the front doors of the lobby were opened, music floated through, and Amanda nodded at them.

The three of them went toward the beach and down the aisle strewn with rose petals. There were so many flowers it looked like a garden had sprung up on the beach. She'd never seen anything so pretty.

Everyone there looked so nice, too, but after a quick sweep of the audience, Jenny's eyes were only on Nick. Handsome, smart, wonderful Nick. His tan suit fit him perfectly. He could have been a model out of a magazine. She laughed and smiled and, just like that, her hand was in his.

"Beautiful," he whispered. "I love you."

She smiled and tried not to cry. "I love you, too."

The vows flew by. Words she would cherish for the rest of her life with him, her heart sailing on the sweet breeze that drifted past. Rings were exchanged, the gold gleaming in the sun.

When the officiant pronounced them husband and wife and Nick kissed her, an enormous cheer went up, far louder than what their small group of family and friends could have produced. Jenny turned to see guests gathered on the beach behind the chairs, applauding.

She and Nick made their way through the raucous crowd of well-wishers and joined the photographer in another tropically landscaped area near the main building for pictures. Rob snapped away, putting them in various poses. A few minutes later, Olivia, Simon, and Yolanda joined them for more pictures.

When the photography was finally done, that part of it anyway, the parents went off to the reception. Nick and Jenny stood back, waiting to be announced.

Jenny held his hand and gazed up at him. "We're married."

He nodded. "We sure are. Went by fast."

"Amanda said it would. But that's okay. We have the rest of our lives together now."

"Yes, we do." He kissed her. "I see your dad showed up."

She swallowed. "I'm glad. I still don't know if he'll really follow through with all of his promises, but that's on him."

Amanda came through the greenery. "Everyone's

seated and ready. I'm going to tell the DJ to announce you, but before I do that, do either of you need anything?"

Jenny looked at Nick and he looked at her. She shook her head. "I have everything I need."

Chapter Forty-three

Olivia had dried her tears in time for the photos with the newly married couple, but it was hard to stop them. Everything was so perfect. Jenny was so beautiful, Nick so handsome. All around her, women were weepy-eyed and dabbing at their faces.

Happy tears, all of them. She glanced at Simon at the other end of the pavilion. He'd almost caused the day to go very differently, because Olivia knew Jenny would have been devastated if he'd made a different decision. She hoped for her daughter's sake that he lived up to the big changes he'd promised.

Eddie brought her a glass of punch from the bar. "You okay?"

She nodded, shifting her attention back to him. She took the beverage he offered. "I'm better than okay. I'm happy. I'm blessed. I'm just trying to take it all in. I want to remember it all just like this."

He smiled. "Today is a great day."

"Yes, it is." She clinked her glass against his and they drank. "I'm so glad you're here with me."

"I wouldn't be anywhere else." He put his arm around her. "Jenny and Nick are about as perfect as can be, eh?"

She could feel tears welling again. "They are," she whispered.

He hugged her and canted his head toward hers. "You're going to make me cry, *mamacita*."

She laughed and turned to kiss him. "You know, that's one of the things I love about you. You're so in touch with your emotions. More so than most men I know. Except maybe Grant. But you're not afraid to let them show. It's such an endearing quality."

Eddie shrugged. "It's the Cuban in me. We are a passionate people."

She pressed against him, enjoying his arms around her, the nearness of him. She loved him so deeply that it often felt to her as though they'd made vows to each other already. "Maybe, someday, you and I should think about...something more permanent."

He grinned. "I think about it all the time. I don't know what you're waiting for."

She shook her head. "You're something else, you know that?"

"Something I hope you plan to keep for a long, long time."

"I do." She meant it, too. With Jenny married, and the question of Simon on the backburner, she felt more available than she ever had before. Freer, somehow. As if now that her daughter was married, Olivia's job as a mother was done.

It wasn't true, of course. She would never stop being Jenny's mom. Never stop being there for her. That wasn't a path any mother stopped walking. And someday, there would hopefully be grandbabies, giving her the new job of grandmother.

But it was as if her future had widened a little, opening up so that there was room for more possibilities for Olivia.

The feeling was a strange one and she didn't quite know what to make of it. She felt like a bird fluttering its wings, trying to decide which way to go. Could she be a wife again? Could she be *Eddie's* wife?

She could. That much she knew. Just like she understood she wasn't necessarily ready to marry Eddie anytime soon, but in a way, it made her feel closer to him. There was a security in what they shared. An understanding that passed beyond a ceremony or a sheet of paper.

"So," he said. "If I were to ask *someday*, you would say yes?"

She nodded. "I would. *Someday*. Not yet. But it doesn't change anything between us, does it? When that happens, I mean? We're so good already. Aren't we?"

"We are. It changes nothing. I know what I want. And it's you."

Her smile returned. "You're such a smooth-talker."

He gestured with his chin toward the dance floor where other couples had begun to float around in circles as a slow, romantic song played. "Dance with me?"

"I'd love to."

They moved around the dance floor, mingling with the others. Olivia's eyes were half-closed with the rightness of it all, until a hand tapped her shoulder. She raised her head to see Jenny and Nick standing beside her and Eddie.

They changed partners, Eddie taking Jenny around for a twirl, while Olivia and Nick took a turn.

"I'm so happy for the two of you," Olivia said. "It was a beautiful ceremony and a perfect day."

"Thank you," he said. "For everything. If not for you, Jenny wouldn't be here, and I never would have met her. I want you to know that I love her more than anything and I'm going to be the best husband I can be to her."

Again, the tears threatened. "I know you will be, Nick. You're a good man. Jenny couldn't have done better. I'm proud to have you as a son-in-law."

"Thanks. Would it be okay if...I called you Mom?"

There was no helping it. A tear slipped out. Olivia sniffed. "Yes, absolutely. I would love that."

She smiled up at him, wondering how she'd been so blessed. But it all came back to one woman. Iris.

She gazed up at Nick again. "Have you danced with Iris?"

"Not yet. But I'm going to. As soon as she's free. Katie's uncle doesn't seem to want to let go of her."

Olivia laughed. "Good for them."

Nick nodded. "I agree. I realize I didn't know my dad that well, unfortunately, but I think he'd like Mr. Hutch. He certainly treats Iris with the kind of respect and admiration that Arthur would have approved of."

"Sadly, I didn't know your dad at all, but what man wouldn't approve of his wife finding happiness again? Look at all Iris has done for so many people. She deserves happiness."

"She does," Nick said. Then he looked at her. "So do you."

Olivia smiled. "I am happy, I promise."

"Does that mean you and Eddie will have a day like this yourselves soon?"

Her smile got even bigger. "I don't know about soon, but we will, someday. I can promise you that we're very committed to each other."

"Good. I like Eddie very much. And I'd think he'd make a great grandfather. When the time comes."

Olivia looked over at Eddie, moving across the dance floor with Jenny. They were both laughing. Eddie had that effect on people. He made them laugh and smile and appreciate life. "He *would* be so good at it." She remembered the word. "*Abuelo*. That's the Spanish word for grandfather."

"*Abuelo*," Nick repeated.

Eddie and Jenny came near them again and they went back to their original partners.

"Jenny's lovely," Eddie whispered into Olivia's. "But I missed you."

Olivia leaned her head against his. "For the five minutes you were away?" But she'd missed him, too. "Maybe...maybe we shouldn't wait too long to make someday happen."

For a moment, his face was blank. Then a slow smile curved his mouth and he nodded, understanding her without any further explanation. "You just say when."

fter Iris had danced with Nick, she finally returned to her seat. A moment later, Emerson appeared with glasses of iced tea for both of them.

"There you are," he said. "I thought I'd lost you to another suitor."

"There's very little chance of that happening."

"I don't know. You've danced with enough men."

She had. So far, Grant, Duke, Owen, and just now, Nick. And she had dances promised to Eddie and David later. "They're all spoken for, I promise."

He smiled as he sat beside her. "Good to know. I'd hate to have to talk to them about putting hands on my girl."

Iris giggled. It had been ages since anyone had acted this way toward her, even if Emerson was just joking. It warmed her up inside. He was so good for her. Until she'd met him, she hadn't realized that she'd wanted this kind of happiness again.

Now that she had it, she recognized that she'd missed it. She'd always thought it was a part of missing Arthur, and it probably was, to some extent. But believing that it was part of missing him had made her think that only Arthur could make her feel like this again.

And clearly, that wasn't true. Emerson was doing a fine job. It was as if a window had been opened in her life and a brand-new breeze had been let in, reminding her that spring was on its way back.

She would never be young again and she was okay with that. But feeling like this made her remember what it was like to be young and that was a very close second.

The music changed to something much more upbeat. Emerson bobbed his head along with the rhythm.

Her fingers went to the Escape Diamond around her neck. What would Arthur think of her new romantic interest? She believed he'd be for it.

She still missed him terribly. She'd give so much to have him back, but that wasn't to be.

She realized Emerson was watching her. Concern filled his gaze. "Are you all right?" he asked. "You look a little sad all of a sudden."

She inhaled. There was no reason not to tell him the truth. There would be no relationship of any kind between them without that. "I was thinking about my late husband."

"Arthur."

She nodded. "I think you two would have been friends."

Emerson thought a moment, then grinned. "Not if he knew I was after you."

She laughed. "You know what I mean."

"I do." He gestured to the diamond around her neck. "He give you that?"

"He did. Although not the way you might think." She explained how the wrapped package had been hidden away in a box in storage and how the girls had found it and brought it to her.

"That was a quite a find."

"So are they," Iris said, looking around the pavilion at all of their beautiful faces. "They saved me. They saved this place. I owe them everything."

"You're a very blessed woman." He reached over and took her hand.

"I am. I know that." She liked the warmth of his hand covering hers. That kind of contact was something else she'd missed. Having it once again was precious.

"I won't be able to give you gifts like that." His gaze was on the diamond.

She turned her hand in his so she could give him a squeeze of reassurance. "I don't need *things*, Emerson. I have all the things I could ever want. And what I don't have, I buy."

She shook her head. "What I need is company. Companionship. Someone to talk to and share experiences with. Someone to laugh with and have a meal with or take a walk on the beach. All the things you're already giving me."

"Good, because I don't have much else."

"That's not true. You have something to give me that Arthur never did."

He made a face. "I do? What is it?"

She smiled. "Music. Arthur had no talents in that area, and it's always been something I've enjoyed very much."

Emerson looked touched by her admission. "I will play for you whenever your heart desires."

"Thank you."

The photographer came over and asked if she and Emerson would join a group photo that had been requested by the mother of the bride.

"Of course," Iris said. "You want both of us?"

"Yes. We're doing the couples."

"All right then," Iris said. She looked at Emerson. "That's us. We're a couple now."

His smile was pure pleasure. "Yes, ma'am."

They followed Rob to a landscaped alcove off to the side. It held a small bench. Nick and Jenny were already seated. Behind them were Olivia and Eddie, Leigh Ann and Grant, Grace and David, Amanda and Duke, and finally, Katie and Owen.

Iris and Emerson stood next to them. Waiting just out of camera shot were Sophie, Gage, Simon, and Yolanda.

Rob gathered them closer together. "In a little more." Then he took a host of photos.

As Iris stood there, Emerson twined his fingers with hers. Her smile got a little bit bigger. A dream was coming true for her. A dream she hadn't even realized she'd had.

She turned her head ever so slightly to see the group around her, her heart overflowing with love and affection.

How had she gotten this second chance at life and love and family? What had she done to deserve this kind of blessing? It was more than she ever could have hoped for.

Tears welled, but she blinked them back. It was the magic of the island. She glanced up. And maybe, it was a little bit of Arthur, looking out for all of them.

She smiled at the blue sky and whispered, "Thank you." A second later, she could have sworn she heard a voice in the breeze saying, "You're welcome."

Not just any voice, but Arthur's. She'd felt him in this place for years. Heard his laugh in the sound of the waves, felt his touch in the gentle breeze, seen the blue of his eyes in the crystal waters.

He would always be with her. Always be a part of this magical island.

And that was exactly how she wanted it.

Want to know when Maggie's next book comes out?
Then don't forget to sign up for her newsletter at her
website!

Also, if you enjoyed the book, please recommend it to a
friend. Even better yet, leave a review and let others
know.

Other Books by Maggie Miller

The Blackbird Beach series:

Gulf Coast Cottage

Gulf Coast Secrets

Gulf Coast Reunion

Gulf Coast Sunsets

Gulf Coast Moonlight

Gulf Coast Promises

Gulf Coast Wedding

Gulf Coast Christmas

About Maggie:

Maggie Miller thinks time off is time best spent at the beach, probably because the beach is her happy place. The sound of the waves is her favorite background music, and the sand between her toes is the best massage she can think of.

When she's not at the beach, she's writing or reading or cooking for her family. All of that stuff called life. She hopes her readers enjoy her books and welcomes them to drop her a line and let her know what they think!

Maggie Online:

www.maggiemillerauthor.com
www.facebook.com/MaggieMillerAuthor

Made in the USA
Middletown, DE
30 December 2022

20845950R00199